SEEKERS

FIRE IN THE SKY

SEEKERS

Also by Erin Hunter

WARRIORS

POWER OF THREE

Book One: The Sight

Book Two: Dark River

Book Three: Outcast

Book Four: Eclipse

Book Five: Long Shadows

Book Six: Sunrise

OMEN OF THE STARS

Book One: The Fourth Apprentice

Book Two: Fading Echoes

EXPLORE THE WARRIORS WORLD

Warriors Super Edition: Firestar's Quest

Warriors Super Edition: Bluestar's Prophecy

Warriors Field Guide: Secrets of the Clans

Warriors: Cats of the Clans

Warriors: Code of the Clans

Warriors: Battles of the Clans

MANGA

The Lost Warrior

Warrior's Refuge

Warrior's Return

The Rise of Scourge

Tigerstar and Sasha #1: Into the Woods

Tigerstar and Sasha #2: Escape from the Forest

Tigerstar and Sasha #3: Return to the Clans

Ravenpaw's Path #1: Shattered Peace

Ravenpaw's Path #2: A Clan in Need

SEEKERS

FIRE IN THE SKY

ERIN
HUNTER

HARPER

AN IMPRINT OF HARPERCOLLINS PUBLISHERS

Fire in the Sky

Copyright © 2010 by Working Partners Limited

Series created by Working Partners Limited

Library of Congress Cataloging-in-Publication Data
Hunter, Erin.
Fire in the sky / by Erin Hunter. — 1st ed.
  p. cm. — (Seekers ; bk. 5)
Summary: Despite their misgivings about the many dangers that lie
ahead, the bears venture out onto the Everlasting Ice and learn of their
final destination with the help of a mystical bear spirit.
ISBN 978-0-06-087134-5 (trade bdg.) — ISBN 978-0-06-087135-2
(lib. bdg.)
  [1. Bears—Fiction. 2. Fantasy.] I. Title.
PZ7.H916625Fir 2010   2009049486
[Fic]—dc22   CIP
                                                              AC

Typography by Hilary Zarycky
10 11 12 13 14   LP/RRDB   10 9 8 7 6 5 4 3 2 1
❖
First Edition

Special thanks to Tui Sutherland

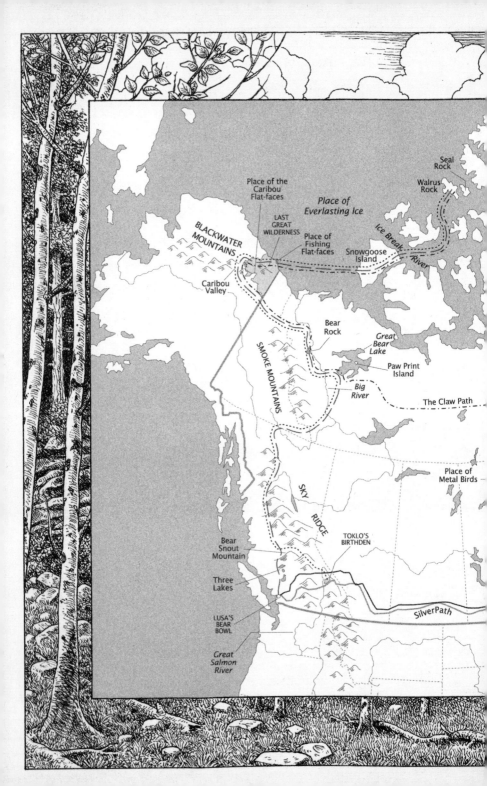

The Bears' Journey: Bear View

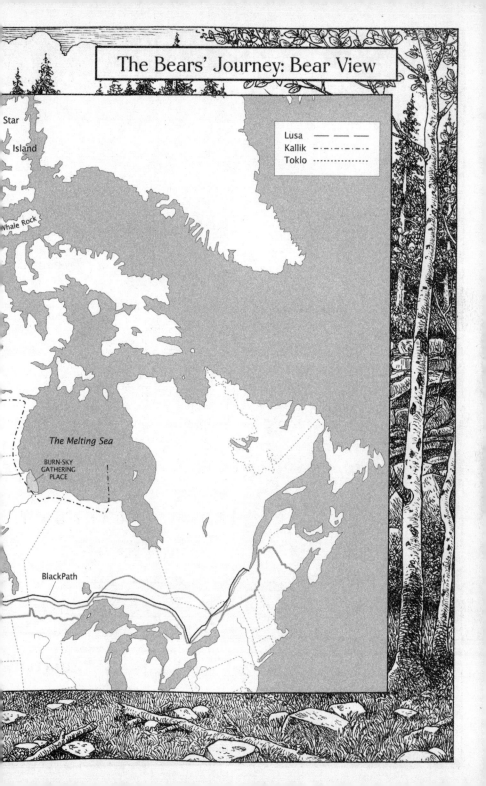

Star

Island

Whale Rock

Lusa	— — —
Kallik	·—·—·—
Toklo	·············

The Melting Sea

BURN-SKY
GATHERING
PLACE

BlackPath

The Bears' Journey: Human View

GREENLAND

ELLESMERE
ISLAND

BAFFIN ISLAND

Godthab

Iqaluit

Atlantic
Ocean

Arctic Circle

Hudson Bay

St. John's

Churchill

WAPUSK
NATIONAL
PARK

Lake
Winnipeg

Quebec

Trans-Canada Highway

Montreal

Winnipeg

Ottawa

Boston

UNITED STATES

St. Paul

Toronto

Minneapolis

New York

CHAPTER ONE

Lusa

Streaks of pink and gold and green flowed across the night sky, stretching long, dazzling clouds of color between the twinkling stars. Rivers of light danced across the bears' fur as they stood on the edge of the shore and watched. They were bathed in waves of cool flame, soundless, touchless, carried in the air like wind. Lusa blinked, her black fur rippling as she shifted on her paws. She'd never seen anything like this before. Nothing in the Bear Bowl had ever been this beautiful, and nothing she'd seen on her long journey with her friends had ever been this strange.

Ujurak must be right. It had to be a sign. The fire in the sky had been sent by the bear spirits, telling them they needed to go onto the ice.

She looked out at the murmuring sea and the vast white emptiness beyond—the Everlasting Ice—and felt a tremor of fear. The rough, pebbly sand under her paws felt solid and comforting. Even though her nose was still clogged with the scent of flat-faces and the sticky black stuff that Ujurak called

1

"oil," she could also smell fresh grass and hear the scrabbling of tiny animals not far away. A tiny splash from the river behind them spoke of fish waiting to be eaten, and even the shadows of the spiky bushes scattered around them promised some shelter from rain or snow.

But out on the ice, there was nothing at all . . . no berries, no grubs, no rabbits, no trees . . . nothing to eat and nowhere to hide, and not even any smells to guide them. Nothing but the cold, empty scent of unmoving water.

How could they save the wild there?

"Ujurak," she said, nudging the small brown bear with her nose. "You are sure about this, aren't you? That is what the sign means . . . that we have to go out *there*?" She nodded her head at the ice.

Ujurak's eyes were dark and serious, with a strange look that suggested he could see things that Lusa never had. "I am sure," he replied. "Kallik must lead us into her world now."

Lusa glanced at their friend. The white bear stood with her snout lifted, inhaling the scents of the ice and the sea as if she couldn't breathe deeply enough. The moonlight turned her fur to dappled silver as the wind brushed across her shoulders. Her muscles quivered with the effort of staying on land when the endless ice tugged at her paws, calling her out. Lusa wished she could understand how Kallik felt. What was there to love about all that emptiness?

She had to be brave, that was all. This quest was bigger than any of them alone, Lusa knew. Maybe it would be more exciting on the ice than she imagined. It would certainly be different from anything she'd seen in the Bear Bowl! "And if we go out there," she asked Ujurak, "we'll be able to save the wild? We can stop the flat-faces from tearing up the land and destroying everything?"

Ujurak bowed his shaggy head and scraped his claws through the sand, leaving deep scars. "I don't know," he confessed. "I don't know what we're supposed to do about the flat-faces, but I do believe that we have to go onto the ice. The fire in the sky has to mean something, I can *feel* it. Even though the land has come to an end, my journey—*our* journey—must continue."

He looked back out at the ice, and Lusa shivered. Although the night wind was bitterly cold, she knew it wasn't the only thing making her skin crawl and her paws tremble.

"Huh!" Toklo's voice snorted behind them. "If you ask me, you've all got bees in your brains." He turned and stalked up the shore toward a line of scraggly bushes.

Oh, no! Lusa thought. They couldn't go without Toklo! The bears had already been separated once, when he decided to go into the mountains on the far side of the plain and lead the life of a lone brown bear. Lusa wasn't exactly sure why he'd come back; she hoped it was because he had changed his mind about leaving them. She'd missed him terribly, and even more than that, she knew that they needed him. All four of them had to save the wild together. It wasn't a coincidence that they'd met and made it so far as a team. Couldn't he see that?

"Toklo, wait!" she called. "What about the fire in the sky? It's not bee-brained—it's a sign!"

Toklo swung his large head around. His black eyes were very bright. "I'm just saying, if we're going on a journey, we'll need to eat something first."

Lusa felt a burst of joy. Toklo was coming with them! Maybe the fire in the sky had affected him more than he wanted to let on. Lusa wasn't exactly sure what Toklo believed about the stars. They didn't seem to fill him with joy, the way they did Lusa and Kallik. But if the stars weren't watching Toklo in a kind way, what did he think they were doing?

She scrambled after him as he padded up the pebbly slope, sniffing the night air.

"Shush," Toklo scolded her. "You'll scare off all the prey."

"Sorry!" Lusa said, trying to tread more lightly. She bumped against his side, resisting the urge to bury her nose in his thick brown fur. "You're so brave, Toklo."

He huffed. "Me?"

"I know you don't have to come," Lusa hurried on. "I mean, I know you'd rather stay on the land . . . but you are really going to come with us, right? Onto the ice?"

Toklo stopped and crouched with his nose to the ground, smelling intently. Lusa pricked up her ears, wondering what he'd sensed. After a long moment, he snorted again.

"Why not?" he muttered, avoiding her eyes. "I mean, the mountain wasn't all *that* great. Too crowded for my liking. Too many bears fighting for too little prey." His shoulders rippled with muscle as he stood up. "Besides, you three would be lost without me." He nudged her teasingly.

"See what I mean?" Lusa said. "You could go off and be on

your own, but instead you're staying with us on this dangerous
journey. That's what I call brave."

Toklo squinted at her, his eyes reflecting the moonlight.
"What about you? You didn't even think twice about following those two. They say, 'Let's go onto the ice!' and right away
you say, 'Where do I put my paws?' If you ask me, you're the
brave one."

"Oh," Lusa said, embarrassed. It seemed different for her;
she couldn't imagine going off and living on her own. Not yet.
She didn't even know if she *could* live on her own. She'd had
to when she first escaped from the Bear Bowl and went to
find Toklo, but she hadn't had a choice about that. And looking for Toklo gave her a purpose, something to think about
beyond surviving. She'd always believed that she'd find him,
so there had always been the thought that she'd have someone
to talk to in the end. But to live entirely alone, with just trees
and ground squirrels for company, wasn't something she could
ever imagine doing. "Well, no," she stammered. "I mean, it's
not like—"

Suddenly there was a flash of motion from the nearest bush
and a rabbit leaped out into the open, tearing away toward
the river. Toklo sprang into action at the same instant and
raced after it with his legs pumping and his belly close to the
ground.

Lusa looked back at the others. Ujurak was climbing the
slope toward her, while Kallik was still standing on the shore
as if she couldn't bear to take one pawstep away from the sea
now that they'd reached it. The shimmering flames of light

in the sky were starting to fade, and the moon was bright and round, casting a silver streak like a path across the water.

She heard a huff of frustration and turned to see Toklo stomping back toward her with no rabbit in his jaws.

"Maybe we'd have better luck over there," Lusa suggested, nodding toward a marshy pool farther along the shore, away from the flat-face bridge. Moonlight glinted off the still water, and there were huddled shadows around it that might be bushes or might be something much more edible. Lusa sniffed eagerly, hoping to catch a scent of prey.

Ujurak brushed against her side and nodded. "I think I smell something over there, too," he murmured.

Kallik caught up to the three of them as they padded quietly toward the pool. She stayed close to Lusa's side, but Lusa could see her large white head swinging around to watch the sea every few paces.

They slowed down as they got closer. A fluttering sound caught Lusa's attention and she froze, holding her breath so she wouldn't scare the prey away. The others looked at her, then back at the pool. The shapes around the pool were geese—a flock of them, all asleep in the long, marshy weeds.

Toklo gave Lusa and Ujurak a look that clearly meant *stay here*. Lusa wondered if he was remembering what had happened the last time they'd hunted for geese. In the thrill of the chase, Ujurak had turned into a big gray bird and had flown away with the flock. When they'd finally found him again, he'd swallowed something terrible and nearly died, and they had to take him to the flat-faces in the hope that they would save him, which was how they had ended up here, so close to the smelly, choking flat-face denning place. Lusa glanced at Ujurak, hoping he wasn't planning to change again. It seemed much safer when he was just a bear, like them.

She settled quietly on the ground next to the young brown bear, watching as Toklo and Kallik split up and crept toward the flock. Pebbly mud squished underneath her, cold against her fur and paw pads, but she had to admit she liked it better than the hard black paths around the flat-face dens. *And it's nowhere near as cold as the ice will be,* she reminded herself, shivering again.

A loud honk abruptly blasted from the flock and several geese lunged upright, taking to the air with ungainly, flapping wings.

"Oh, no!" Lusa cried, sitting up. "Did they all get away?"

"No, look," Ujurak said. He nodded at the brown and white shapes of Toklo and Kallik as they leaped into the mass of wings and feathers, claws outstretched. When the rest of the geese had disappeared into the dark sky, Lusa could see both of her friends trotting toward them triumphantly, each dragging a fat goose carcass.

"Great catch!" she yelped, bouncing down to join them.

Kallik shrugged modestly.

"As if a fat bird like this could escape from a decent hunter," Toklo scoffed, dropping the goose and tossing his head.

The four bears settled down by the pond, next to a clump of bushes that blocked the cold wind, and tore into the juicy flesh of the geese. Lusa was surprised to realize how tired she was. Now that she had sat down, she didn't think she could get up again. She was glad for the chance to rest her paws and aching muscles.

The crunch of bones and meat in her mouth helped to revive her a little. She gazed into the still water next to them and saw large shapes reflected in the moonlight. It took her a moment to realize she was looking at herself and her friends. She was so much bigger than she remembered! Her fur was thick and dark and her ears were larger than the last time she'd seen herself in a pool of water. She always felt so small next to the others. Toklo seemed stronger and taller every day, and Kallik was even larger than he was.

Lusa glanced at the white bear. Kallik's massive jaws pulped the rich goose fat, while her long claws ripped off another chunk of meat. If Lusa hadn't known Kallik all along, she would probably be terrified to run into her now. A full-grown white bear might even *eat* a smaller black bear like Lusa!

Just as she had that thought, a goose feather drifted up Kallik's nose, and the white bear jumped back and sneezed loudly. She sneezed again, and then again, and her expression was so startled and outraged that Lusa couldn't help letting out a huff of laughter. Maybe Kallik wasn't so scary after all.

"Let's find somewhere dry to sleep," Toklo suggested once the geese were picked clean.

"Yes! Sleep!" Lusa agreed, pushing herself to her paws. She felt strangely heavy, as if her pelt was soaking wet. The others gave her funny looks, but she couldn't think of anything she'd rather do right then than curl up somewhere warm to nap.

"What about the ice?" Kallik said. "Shouldn't we get started? We could sleep out there."

That didn't sound warm and cozy to Lusa. How could any bear fall asleep on the ice?

"That's a stupid idea," Toklo snorted, as if he'd read Lusa's mind. "This is probably our last chance to get a decent night's sleep."

"What's that supposed to mean?" Kallik flared. "We'll sleep fine out there! Better even, because we won't have dirt clogging up our fur or no-claws stomping around and nearly running us over with their firebeasts!"

"Oh, sure," Toklo said. "I bet it's *really* comfortable sleeping on solid frozen water. I can't *wait*."

Lusa's ears twitched. Privately she agreed with Toklo, but she thought he was being unfair to Kallik. After all, this was the place she had longed to find—where all white bears dreamed of living because the ice stayed forever. If white bears could survive out there, so could they. They needed to trust Kallik to keep them safe, that was all.

"Hey!" Kallik growled. "I don't complain about the nasty hot dirty places *you* find for us to sleep—"

"Okay, all right, that's enough," Ujurak interrupted, shouldering his way between them before Toklo could lash out at Kallik with his claws. With a shock, Lusa realized that Ujurak was almost as broad as Toklo now, and his fluffy cub pelt was giving way to blond streaks of coarser hair, like a full-grown grizzly. "Listen, we need to rest before we start, especially if we'll have to swim to reach the ice."

"Yeah," Toklo said smugly.

"Although I'm sure we'll also be very comfortable sleeping on the ice like Kallik does," Ujurak added, giving Toklo a warning look.

"I guess it would be a good idea to get some rest first," Kallik admitted, flicking her stumpy tail.

"Besides, Lusa looks like she's about to fall asleep on her paws," Toklo joked.

"I am n—" Lusa's protest was cut short by a huge yawn. "Okay, maybe I am," she muttered as the others huffed with amusement. They wouldn't think it was funny if they felt as tired as she did. She was relieved to see Toklo's fur settling back down on his shoulders, and when she stumbled against Kallik's flank because her paws wouldn't lift up properly, the white bear nuzzled her with a friendly snort. Though she'd never admit it out loud, it scared Lusa when Kallik and Toklo confronted each other like that; then it was too easy to see the strength in their shoulders, and the glint of their hooked claws. Lusa hoped the two of them wouldn't quarrel when they got to the ice. Once Toklo realized that Kallik knew what she was doing, everything would be all right.

They headed up the slope away from the sea, looking for dry grass and shelter from the wind. The pebbly sand underpaw gave way to tufts of thick grass. Beyond the river, Lusa could see a line of trees up on a ridge. She could almost hear their leaves rustling from here. She wished she could curl up in their safe, strong branches, or tuck herself between their thick roots. She wanted to fall asleep surrounded by the whispers of bear spirits watching over her from behind the bark.

One thing she knew for sure: There were no trees on the ice. No trees meant no friendly black bear spirits. What if she died out in the cold, white emptiness? Would her spirit ever find its way back where it belonged?

"It's all right," said a gruff voice in her ear. Lusa turned and saw Toklo padding along beside her. Kallik and Ujurak were a few pawsteps ahead. Toklo nodded at the wooded ridge. "I know you wish you were up there."

"You're right. Which means that I'm not brave at all," Lusa said. "Toklo, I'm terrified."

"Well, all of us are," Toklo grunted. Lusa tilted her head in surprise. "I mean, I'm not *very* scared," he amended. "Just a little bit. Only because it's squirrel-brained to leave the land, where all the prey and shelter are. Brown and black bears don't belong on the ice. But I figure we have to trust Ujurak. He's led us all the way here, and we're still in one piece."

"Yes," Lusa murmured, turning her gaze to the shambling bulk of the shape-shifting bear ahead of them. "He hasn't let us down so far."

"There's not enough room to be a bear on land anymore," Toklo went on in a low growl. His eyes were focused on the dark, blurred line of mountains on the horizon. "Perhaps there will be room for us out there, on the empty ice." He snorted. "There *should* be room. There isn't anything *else* out there."

Lusa was about to tell him she'd been thinking the same thing, when something pale and warm loomed ahead of her, and she collided with Kallik's haunches. The white bear had stopped with Ujurak beside a clump of thornbushes. Ujurak was nosing around them, checking for prickles in the grass, or sharp-edged stones, or anything else that would make this a bad place to rest for the night. Lusa was beyond caring; she was so tired, she imagined she could sleep quite comfortably on a BlackPath.

She felt a flash of anxiety that Kallik had overheard her and Toklo worrying about the ice.

"I can't wait to see your home," she whispered, pressing her nose into the white bear's fur. That was true—she did want to understand where her friend came from, even if it frightened her.

Kallik nuzzled her gently. "You're going to love it, Lusa," she promised. "You'll see. No firebeasts, no smoke, no oil. Nothing to tempt the no-claws out there. Just you and the wind and the feeling of cool under your paws. It's the best place ever."

Lusa didn't argue, but right then she would have thought anywhere she could close her eyes was the best place ever. The grass here was tall and soft, and the bushes hid them from the strong gusts of wind off the sea, as long as they didn't get close enough to the branches for the thorns to stab them. Small flecks of white drifted through the air, glimmering in the moonlight. It was starting to snow. In Lusa's fuzzy head, it just seemed like a soft, cozy blanket settling on her fur.

She flopped down, and by the time the others were settled snugly around her, she was fast asleep.

* * *

A murmur of chattering voices surrounded her, too high and fast for her to understand. Lusa pawed at her eyes and sat up, then stopped with a gasp.

Flat-faces!

Lots and lots of flat-faces were peering down at her, their pale, furless faces blank.

Lusa spun around to wake up her friends and realized they were gone. Gone also were the thornbushes and the smell of the sea, replaced by sloping gray walls and a tall, familiar tree with wide-spaced branches, and a group of bears she'd never expected to see again.

She was in the Bear Bowl. Lusa relaxed, letting the tension out of her shoulders. This was just a dream. She'd visited the Bear Bowl in her sleep once before, when she'd been told to save the wild. Nothing to be scared of, just her mind wandering through her memories. There hadn't been so many flat-faces in her last dream. Lusa stood up on her hindpaws to look at them. She remembered how they used to point at her and laugh in their high, chattering way when she danced— especially the flat-face cubs. She tried waving her paws and wiggling her snout in the air. Maybe they would throw her blueberries if she did that. Even dream blueberries would be better than none.

But the flat-faces just stared at her in silence. Their faces were as blank and cold as the stone gray walls. They didn't care what she did.

Lusa dropped to her paws. "Hrrrmph," she muttered. "Well, I don't care about you, either." She turned her back on them, trying to hide the uneasy shiver that went through her fur.

"Don't worry about them," said her mother's gentle voice. Ashia pressed up next to Lusa, sniffing her from ears to paws. "You're still not eating enough, little one. Look how thin you are!"

"We're eating better in the Last Great Wilderness, though," Lusa pointed out. She bumped her mother under her chin. "I am a wild bear, after all. I had goose tonight!"

"Really? I've never had that," her mother said. "I know you have traveled far, far away, but sometimes I wish you were still here, playing with Yogi, listening to Stella's stories, sleeping in the curl of my belly." Sadness filled Ashia's brown eyes. "The wild needs you, I know that, but you will always be my precious cub, and I will never forget it."

"I know," Lusa whispered. "I miss you, too." She looked over to the rocks where King was sunning himself while Yogi toyed with a dead leaf. Yogi looked much bigger than she remembered, and his coat was turning sleek and long instead of tufty and fuzzy around his ears.

"We'll see each other in our dreams," Ashia went on. "I'm very proud of you, little blackberry. I know you're going to save the wild."

Lusa stretched her paws out in front of her, feeling sleepy again. "We will try," she promised. She started circling in the grass, digging up a comfortable nest. "I'd better get some more sleep," she grunted. "I don't know why I'm so tired."

"Wait," Ashia yelped, looking concerned. She nudged Lusa's side as Lusa lay down. "Stay awake. Lusa, don't fall asleep. You can't go to sleep yet."

Lusa blinked at her. "But I'm so tired," she protested, feeling like a tiny cub again, too weak to play outside the den for long. She snuggled up to her mother's strong, furry legs. "Just let me sleep for a little while."

The Bear Bowl started to fade around her. "Lusa!" her mother's voice called again, sounding farther and farther away. "Lusa, you must stay awake. It's very important. Lusa!"

CHAPTER TWO

Kallik

The clear, crisp smell of ice wove its way into Kallik's dreams. Her legs churned as she raced across a skylength of snow, as fast and strong as her mother, Nisa, had once been. Her brother, Taqqiq, bounded along beside her, barking at her to keep up, to race him to the seal hole where food waited, warm and salty smelling, pulsing with juicy fat. . . .

When Kallik woke up, the scent was still in her nose, calling her toward the ocean. It smelled closer than ever. She pushed herself to her paws, shaking off the cold morning dew. Toklo was already awake, splashing quietly through the river with his eyes fixed on the ripples, watching for fish. Ujurak was stirring as if he was about to wake up, while Lusa looked so fast asleep that Kallik bent down to make sure she was still breathing. In her sleep, Lusa muttered, "Hrrmmmrrrgerroff," and rolled away from Kallik.

Shaking her head in amusement, Kallik padded toward the shore. Her paws sped up as she scrambled across the shingle, running to the water and the ice she could smell in the distance.

The scent of it was so strong that she almost expected to see a sheet of pure white ice reaching all the way to the shore, but the sea closest to them was still not yet frozen. Foam-dappled waves brushed against the sand with a murmuring sound like spirits whispering.

Kallik peered out to the horizon, squinting in the grayish morning light. The rising sun was partly hidden by a thin veil of mist, with streaks of golden light peeking through in pale glimmers on the water. The mist hung low over the ocean as well, but Kallik padded along the shore until she found the spot where the ice smelled strongest. It couldn't be far to get to the ice from here. Just a short swim away . . . and then she'd have ice under her paws again!

"You are way too excited about this," Toklo grunted as he stalked up behind her and dropped a large fish on the sand. "We're not all white bears, remember. I hope you know what you're doing, taking us all out there." He turned and let out an impatient growl as Ujurak and Lusa wandered slowly up behind him. Ujurak was carrying two smaller fish. Lusa was shaking her head as if her ears were full of water, and was pawing sleepily at her muzzle.

"Come on, hurry up, snailpaws," Toklo growled at Lusa. He poked her in the side with his nose. "Where's all that annoying early-morning cheerfulness you're usually so full of?"

"Well, maybe if you hadn't woken me up by dropping a *fish* on my head," Lusa protested, yawning.

"It's a good big fish," Toklo said proudly. He jabbed his newkill with a paw. "We'd better eat while we still can."

Kallik felt her shoulder fur rising. "There's prey out on the ice, too!" she barked. "Really good prey! Just you wait until I catch you a seal!"

"Sure," Toklo muttered as he ripped off a chunk of fish. "I'll wait for that."

"We'll be fine out there," Lusa interjected quickly. "Ujurak's excited, too—right, Ujurak?"

The small brown bear was standing with his front paws in the water, gazing quietly out at the horizon. "Is this the way we have to go?" he asked Kallik.

Kallik swallowed. That was the kind of question Ujurak usually had the answer to—not her! But she was supposed to lead them to the ice, and she didn't want Toklo or Lusa to worry that she couldn't do it. So she tried to sound confident as she replied, "Yes, there's ice right out there. I can smell it." She lifted her nose to inhale the beautiful clean scent. "I'm sure we can swim to it. It isn't far at all."

"Swim to it?" Lusa echoed, licking the last bits of fish off her fur. She padded over to stand beside Ujurak and dabbed her paw in the water. "*Brrr!* It's very cold!"

"Well, of course," Kallik said. "Otherwise it couldn't have ice on it, could it?"

"And it tastes funny," Toklo said suspiciously, dipping his snout in the water. He stuck out his tongue and pawed at it with a disgusted look. "*Blech!* That's not normal water at all!"

"No, it's salty," Kallik said, hanging on to her patience. "You don't drink it, you swim in it. Look, it's no different from swimming in the Big River. Remember? We did that just fine, and this is a shorter distance."

Toklo squinted into the mist. "How can you tell?"

"I trust Kallik's nose," Ujurak said quietly, before Kallik lost her temper and shoved Toklo into the ocean. "This is the way for us."

The bears finished off the large fish, although Kallik could barely eat; her head was full of seals and of snow crunching underpaw and of cold, sharp winds that lifted her pelt, hair by hair. She hoped that Taqqiq had found ice somewhere, too. She wanted to think of him hunting seals and rolling in snow . . . just like she would be soon! Toklo noisily swiped his tongue around his muzzle. Ujurak was using his teeth to scrape fish scales from under his claws. Lusa was standing still, her head bobbing as if she was falling asleep again.

"Are we ready?" Kallik prompted. This was it; the moment she had journeyed all this way for. It seemed so long since she had been on solid ice that for a heartbeat she couldn't remember what it felt like. Nisa had been alive, and she and Taqqiq had been helpless cubs, pretending to be brave when really they knew nothing about how to survive. . . .

"Are we going, or are you waiting for the ice to come to us?" Toklo snapped.

Kallik jumped. "Sorry, just . . . just thinking. Come on, keep together. There will be stronger currents in this water than in the river or the lake. Don't get swept away. If you feel yourself drifting, paddle into the current and it should bring you back to where you started."

Lusa padded close to Kallik's side as they waded into the

water. She jumped back in surprise when a wave rolled in toward her, but Kallik nudged her forward. She could see Lusa's paws trembling, but the little black bear didn't turn back.

The cold, salty tang of the ocean air tingled in Kallik's nose. "Stay close to me, and I'll help you if you need it, all right?"

Lusa nodded, her eyes wide.

"Blech!" Toklo complained behind them. Kallik could hear him splashing loudly and batting at his nose. "What if we swallow this stuff? It's so gross!"

"It's just water, Toklo," she called back. "Sheesh," she muttered, and beside her Lusa snorted with amusement.

"Oh, wow," Ujurak said, leaning down to sniff the waves as they surged around his paws. "I can sense so many animals out there in the sea! Animals, and fish, and animals that look like fish but aren't . . ."

"Well, don't change *now*," Toklo grumbled. "We might never find you again."

Then even Toklo had to shut up, because they'd waded in far enough for the water to splash over their muzzles. Kallik pushed off from the gravelly, sandy bottom and started to swim. The water lifted and tugged on her fur and her paws churned as she shoved herself forward. She felt a burst of happiness as the sea buoyed her up and waves rolled under her body. It was as if the water was welcoming her back into the world of white bears; this was where she was meant to be. The heaviness she always felt on land drifted away, leaving her weightless and full of strength. The river had been dirty, sucking her down into its black depths, but this empty gray water let her slice cleanly through, and even the waves didn't seem to be trying to push her back to the shore.

Kallik kept an eye on the small black shape of Lusa's head, only a few pawlengths away. Lusa's snout stuck up in the air and she gasped for breath as she paddled, but if Kallik went slowly, she could keep up. The brown bears were close behind them, swimming vigorously. Toklo closed his eyes every time a wave came toward him, and when it swamped over his head he poked his muzzle out the other side, sputtering and snorting.

Soon Kallik's muscles began to ache; she hadn't used them for swimming like this in a while. She knew that if *she* was tired, Lusa must be even more so. The little black bear had seemed much quieter recently, and cheerful only when they made their nests for the night. Had the long journey tired Lusa out? Kallik wondered how much farther they would have to go. Even Ujurak seemed unsure. And the ice was still a long way distant—a shimmering blue shelf at the edge of the sky up ahead.

"Lusa!" she called. "You can rest your paws and float for a moment, if you want. Look." She stopped paddling and let her paws hang. The salty water kept her afloat, with only a flick of her paws needed now and then to keep her head above water.

"I'll try," Lusa burbled as water went up her nose. She coughed and flailed, then kept her legs still and quiet below the surface of the water, the way Kallik had. Her look of surprised relief made Kallik feel warm inside.

She paddled back to Toklo and Ujurak to give them the same advice, and for a while all four bears drifted calmly, catching their breath and resting their sore muscles. Beneath the water, Kallik felt more alive than ever, even though she wasn't moving. She could tell from the way the current brushed against her fur which way they needed to swim, and she knew exactly where her companions were from the tiny ripples they sent out when they moved their paws to keep afloat. It was like being able to *see* without putting her head underwater.

"*SQUAWK!*" shrieked a bird overhead. "*SQUAWK! SQUAWK!*" A seagull plummeted toward them, diving straight for Kallik. Its sharp yellow beak just missed her nose, and Kallik let out a roar, swiping at it with her front paws. But the gray-and-white bird swooped away and hovered on a current of air just out of reach. Kallik thought it looked very smug.

"Just you try that again!" she challenged, bobbing up and down in the waves she'd created.

"*SQUAWK!*" it hollered back. Kallik glared as the bird circled overhead. It was clearly waiting until she stopped paying attention to it, and then it would come back to annoy her some more.

"Stupid seagulls," she muttered, just as the bird swooped down again. This time it aimed for Ujurak's nose, and the small brown bear ducked under the water to escape.

"Go away!" Kallik barked. "Or we'll eat you!"

"*SQUAW-AW-AW-AW-AWK!*" the seagull cackled. It flew up in a wide arc, then dove back down toward Toklo.

"Uh-oh. Now it's messing with the wrong bear," Lusa

puffed, churning her paws to lift her head higher above the waves. Toklo surged out of the water right at the lowest point of the bird's dive and swiped his claws at it. The hooked tips grazed the seagull's feathers and nearly dragged the bird into the sea. It was almost upside down before it managed to right itself with a panicky thrust of its wings. It flapped out of reach of Toklo in an awkward, unbalanced way, scattering feathers.

"SQUAAAAAAAAWK!" it screeched in outrage, then turned and flew away.

"That's right!" Kallik called after it. "Pick on someone your own size!"

"I think I'm ready to keep swimming," Lusa said, taking a deep breath. Kallik paddled closer to her, and they all began to swim again. It was much colder than the Big River. Kallik could feel the piercing chill even through her thick fur; she knew Lusa's paws must be nearly numb by now. Craning her neck, she saw a jagged white ledge looming above the waves. *The Endless Ice!* She'd finally found it. Far, far from her Birth-Den, she was safe once more.

"Almost there," she barked encouragingly as the ice shelf drew closer. "We're so close!" The pure white ledge ahead of them was like the promise of newkill after a hunt. Kallik could almost taste it. She put on a burst of speed across the last stretch of water and hauled herself up, hooking her claws in the ridges of the shelf. With a fierce, wriggling push, she scrambled out of the water and sprawled out onto the flat expanse of ice.

It was deliciously cold underneath her. Her paws felt cool and light instead of heavy and caked with mud, as they had for the last several moons. She wanted to roll and leap and rub her back into the snow, breathing in the clean, icy air.

But first she turned around to help Lusa up. Gently she put her jaws around the scruff at the back of Lusa's neck and tugged her upward, as Nisa used to do with her and Taqqiq. Lusa yelped with shock as her paws skidded across the ice and she landed in a small, wet heap at Kallik's paws.

"*Brrrrrrrrrrrrrrrrrrrr!*" Lusa cried, shaking herself and spraying drops of water all over Kallik. "How can it be even colder when I'm out of the water? *Brrr! Brrrr! BRRRR!*" She scrambled up and tried turning in circles to warm herself up, but her paws kept slipping on the slippery ice until she tumbled onto her side or her belly.

Toklo boosted Ujurak up and then let Kallik help him out of the water. Both brown bears immediately slipped and scrabbled across the ice, crashing into Lusa and ending up in a wet pile of fur. Lusa whoomphed with amusement from underneath Toklo.

"It's a little slippery," Kallik said, realizing she should have warned them.

"Oh, *is it?*" Toklo roared.

"You just have to move slowly at first!" Kallik said. She hurried over to untangle her friends.

"I can't even stand up!" Toklo grumbled, thudding onto his side again. He collected his paws underneath him, braced himself, and tried to shove himself upright. Immediately all four paws shot in different directions and he sprawled face-first onto the ice.

"I'm glad you think this is so funny!" he huffed at Lusa, who was rolling in the snow, chuffing with laughter. "How are we supposed to travel if we can't even walk?"

"You'll get used to it," Kallik promised. She leaned against him to support him until he was standing upright, looking wobbly. "Here, spread out your paws and slide them one at a time, like this. Focus on keeping your balance lower than your belly, so that you're almost bending your legs." She leaned from one side to the other and skated across the ice. It felt so natural to her that for a moment she was a cub again, and she looked back to see if her mother was watching. But there were no white bears here, just three bedraggled heaps of dark fur with huge baleful eyes and dripping muzzles.

Toklo looked unimpressed. *"Hmmph,"* he grumbled. "Stupid ice." He tried to slide forward a step like Kallik had and ended up sprawled on his face again.

Kallik winced. "It also helps if you find rougher patches of ice to walk on, or fresh snow. Those are less slippery, and you can sink your claws in a bit more."

Ujurak skated over to her side, looking only a little unbalanced. Kallik wondered if he could use white bear skills without actually becoming a white bear. He certainly seemed to learn the fastest.

"We'll get used to it," he said, inhaling the cold, sharp air. "We just need to practice. Let's keep walking while it's still light."

"That'll warm us up, too," Lusa said through chattering teeth. She yawned and shivered.

"Come on, sleepyhead," said Toklo, nudging her.

Lusa didn't move. "But how do we know where to go?" she whispered. She gazed at the vast stretch of white ice that surrounded them on three sides. "There are no paths to follow. I can't even smell anything, my nose is so cold!"

"Mine, too!" Toklo snorted. He pawed at his snout. "Or maybe there isn't anything to smell out here."

"Are you serious?" Kallik said. She took a deep breath and closed her eyes. "I can smell the sea, and the scent of snow on its way, and the beating warmth of seals waiting for me to catch them, and somewhere far away, other white bears hunting." She opened her eyes, but her friends were staring at her blankly. "There are all kinds of signs to read on the ice, just like on land," she insisted. "Right, Ujurak?"

"Sure," he said, a little hesitantly. "I mean . . . I understand the land signs better, but that's all right, because we have you to read the ice signs."

That made Kallik a little nervous. "But you'll tell me if we're going the wrong way, right?" she asked. "I mean, I don't know where we're supposed to end up or anything like that."

"Don't worry," Ujurak reassured her. "Just follow your instincts. Do what you would normally do on the ice. I'm sure our path will become clear as we travel."

Kallik wasn't entirely convinced. She wanted to show her friends the amazing world of the ice . . . but she didn't want to be the one responsible for finding whatever it was Ujurak thought they were looking for. She didn't want it to be her fault if they failed to save the wild.

Lusa lifted one front paw, then the other, peering at the smooth surface underneath her. "It looks so empty," she said.

"It's not empty at all!" Kallik insisted, pushing aside her worries. "Look more closely. What do you see?"

All four bears dipped their heads to stare into the ice.

"I see ice," Toklo growled after a moment.

Kallik sighed.

"Bubbles!" Lusa said suddenly. "And . . . and shadows, maybe? It's like something is moving inside the ice." She edged sideways, looking nervous.

"Exactly!" Kallik cried. "Those are the spirits of dead bears."

Lusa didn't look reassured.

"Great," Toklo snorted. "Dead bubbly bears."

"No, you don't understand. They are there to guide me like your spirits guide you in the trees, Lusa, or you in the water, Toklo," Kallik persisted. "They're always there, just under your paws, and they show you where the ice is too thin to walk. Sometimes they guide you to the breathing holes of seals, or warn you about danger ahead." Kallik licked her lips, her mouth watering with anticipation. "You'll love the taste of seals. Just wait till I catch one!"

"All right, enough talk," Toklo grumbled. "Lead the way."

Kallik turned and faced the horizon. She was home! This was her world, and now she could show her friends how wonderful it was. She just had to trust that the ice spirits would guide them to their destination, as Ujurak's spirits had been guiding him.

She took a deep breath, searching the air for useful smells. Was the seal smell in this direction? It had been so long since she'd smelled it . . . but the warm, rich, fatty scent made her hungry, even though she could tell it was far away.

She looked down at the bubbles, hoping they would guide her the way her mother had taught her they would. It seemed as if there were a lot more spirit-bubbles and shadows than she remembered from her childhood on the ice with Nisa. Was she remembering wrong . . . or was the ice different here? There was less white around the spirit-bubbles, so the ice looked almost black in places. As if it was hardly there at all . . .

A chilly breeze rippled through Kallik's fur. Did that mean lots of white bears had died since she'd last stood on the ice? She thought of all the white bears at Great Bear Lake, heading back toward the rising sun, like Taqqiq. What if they hadn't made it back to the Melting Sea? Or what if they had made it back, but it hadn't frozen? They couldn't have survived forever eating leaves and twigs.

What if one of these ice spirits was her own brother? How would she ever know?

Stop worrying, she told herself, shaking her head. *This is where you're supposed to be! You made it back to the ice!*

Thrumming with excitement, she shoved the anxious thoughts out of her mind and padded toward the seal smell, leading the others out into the icy expanse.

CHAPTER THREE

Kallik

As they left the water behind them, the ice became less liquid under their paws, and Kallik found more gritty patches for them to walk on without slipping. White hills of snow surrounded them, piled into whorls and crests by the force of the wind. Some of the snowdrifts were higher than Kallik if she'd been standing upright on her back paws; others were barely squirrel-sized mounds. She kept an eye out for other white bears, but she smelled only one or two in the distance, and the falling snow hid any prints that might have been left behind. Once she thought she scented a dead seal, but when she found it, the carcass had been picked clean of any flesh and there was nothing left to eat.

More snow began to fall, whirling white powder drifting down from the sky and balancing on the surface of the ice, too light to land properly. Kallik almost imagined she could see her mother and brother walking ahead of her in a swirl of the storm. Right now Nisa would be telling them stories of Sila-luk, while Taqqiq tried to wrestle Kallik into the snow.

"Great Spirits, this is boring," Toklo announced suddenly.

Kallik jumped, distracted from her memories. "Boring?" she echoed.

The brown bear scuffed at the snow under his paws. "There's nothing to smell, nothing to see, nothing to chase. Nothing but white, white, white in every direction."

"I think it's pretty," Lusa said loyally.

"And there's so *much* to see!" Kallik said. "Every snowdrift is different. Every block of ice has a unique shape, and it's not even all white. . . . Look at this one." She padded over and tapped a large outcropping of ice with one of her claws. A few sparkling shards broke off and landed in the snow. "Can't you see all the shades of blue and gray and white in there? It's like a rainbow, but even more beautiful."

"I can see them," Ujurak agreed, peering over his nose at the ice.

Toklo looked skeptical. "So that's what you do out here?" he said. "Stare at the ice? That sounds like fun."

"We play games, too!" Kallik protested. "Taqqiq and I played the best games! Watch." She spun around and saw Lusa still gazing intently at the ice block, looking for blue reflections.

"WALRUS ATTACK!" Kallik suddenly bellowed, throwing herself into the snow beside Lusa.

"Where?" Lusa shrieked. She leaped back and whirled around, her eyes wild and terrified. "What's a walrus? Where is it? Why can't I see it?"

"No, no, no," Kallik said, woofing with laughter. "It's a

game. I'm sorry, I didn't mean to scare you. Taqqiq and I used to play this all the time."

"Oh," said Lusa. She sounded more bewildered than amused.

"So one of us is the walrus—let's say Toklo," Kallik offered. Toklo tossed his head and made a face that he probably thought was walrus-y. "And then as we're walking along, all of a sudden he jumps up and yells, 'Walrus attack!' and chases one of us. If he catches you, then you're the next walrus. Make sense?"

"Um . . . okay," Lusa said.

"It's fun!" Kallik insisted, scrambling up and shaking snowflakes from her ears. She swiped a pawful of snow at Lusa.

"Yikes!" Lusa yelped as the snow splattered across her ears. At least it seemed to wake her up. "You'll be sorry now!" she cried, scooping up her own lump of snow and flinging it at Kallik.

Kallik dodged and galloped out of reach. A pleased chortle rumbled in her throat. But it died when she looked back at the two brown bears: Ujurak trudging along blinded and deafened by his secret thoughts, and Toklo barely keeping his paws under him and growling at every step.

"If you keep acting like cubs, we'll never get anywhere before nightfall," he grumbled. "I'd rather find food than play a silly game."

Kallik swallowed. Toklo was right. This wasn't like her and Taqqiq playing outside their den. Now she had to be like Nisa, keeping the others safe and alive.

"All right, we'll just keep walking," she said. "I smell seal up ahead." She looked up at the sky and realized that the snow was falling faster, covering the ice more thickly and adding to the drifts in fragile layers that hadn't yet been carved by the wind.

"*I* don't smell anything," Toklo answered petulantly, but he pawed snow out of his eyes and followed her without any more arguing.

They walked for a long time across a landscape that probably looked unchanging to the others, but to Kallik's eyes showed clear signs that they were getting farther from the water and nearer the thicker parts of the ice: Their pawsteps made dull thuds on the ground rather than slippery whispers, and the ridges of snow were set like rock at the base, worn down by the wind over uncountable seasons. Some of the snow was so hard that Kallik wondered if it had *ever* melted. Were the stories about the Everlasting Ice true—that it stayed frozen forever? Kallik's heart sang. *I found it, Nisa, Taqqiq! I had faith, and I found it!*

But only she belonged here. Not her companions, with their different-colored fur. As her paws began to ache, Kallik looked back at Lusa, trudging through the snow at a snail's pace. Toklo walked beside her, glancing at her anxiously. Ujurak was right behind them. Kallik checked the sky again. The sun was starting to sink below the white horizon. It wasn't late enough for Kallik to feel tired, but the days were shorter than the nights now, which meant less time for hunting, and longer without the warmth of the sun. Lusa was shivering even more as the air grew colder.

Kallik stopped, thinking: *What would Nisa do now?* She could smell the seal not far away, but it would still be a while before they reached it, especially at the pace of the other three bears.

"The days are getting a lot shorter," Ujurak observed quietly, catching up to her. "The sun is leaving, and earthsleep is coming."

"I'm hungry," Toklo snapped. His shaggy head turned to Kallik. A dusting of snow through his brown fur made him look strangely mottled. "Do your spirit-bubbles have any thoughts on how much farther it is to this seal?"

Kallik pressed herself up to Lusa. The little black bear was swaying on her paws, her eyes rolling with exhaustion. "I think it's more important to find shelter now," Kallik said. "I'll hunt first thing tomorrow."

"Shelter!" Toklo barked, looking around. "There is no shelter out here!"

"Maybe not the kind you're used to," Kallik said. "But here . . . this will work." She led the way over to a tall mound of compacted snow, a few pawlengths higher than her head. She tried to remember how Nisa had built their dens. Working steadily, she scooped out pawfuls of snow, packing down the sides so it didn't collapse in. Soon she had hollowed out a cave in the snow, just big enough for the four of them.

Lusa tilted her head doubtfully. "We're going to sleep *inside* the snow?" she said. "That sounds . . . freezing."

"No, it's lovely and warm," Kallik reassured her. "And you'll be out of the wind. Trust me."

Lusa didn't argue. She climbed inside the cave and curled up in the center, away from the snowy walls. Kallik followed her in and bundled up beside her, trying to share as much of her warmth as she could. She didn't feel the cold at all yet. To her, it was a relief not to be hot, not to have dirt clinging to her paws all the time.

Toklo and Ujurak squeezed in next to them until the small space was full of fur. Kallik scraped snow across the entrance until they were neatly tucked in. The heat from their bodies warmed the air inside the cave quickly.

"Today was fun," Lusa murmured sleepily. "I like your ice, Kallik."

Kallik had a feeling Lusa was just being kind, but she nuzzled her friend's side in appreciation.

"I guess it is warm enough in here," Toklo snorted, resting his head on Lusa's back. "Surprisingly."

Kallik felt Ujurak's snout flop across her back paws, and Lusa's ears flicking next to her chin. As she drifted off to sleep, listening to the storm grow stronger outside, she thought of the bear spirits dancing in the sky above them. Like the spirits under their paws, the ones in the sky would watch over them as well.

This was right. The ice was where they were meant to be.

The next morning dawned bright and clear. The snowstorm had passed, leaving drifts of sparkling snow across the ice and a brilliant blue sky overhead. Kallik shouldered her way out of the cave, shaking snow off her paws. She took a deep breath. It was beautiful. How could the others not love it here?

"I'm still hungry," Toklo grumbled from inside the make-shift den. "Lusa, would you wake up already?"

Kallik peeked back in and saw him prodding the sleeping black bear with his paw. Ujurak joined in, nosing her from the other side, until Lusa finally blinked awake and rubbed her snout.

"Great thistles, you're like bees in my fur," she complained to the brown bears. "Can't I sleep just a bit longer?" She buried her head in her paws again.

"No!" Toklo barked, shoving her with his muzzle. "I'm hungry! Get up so we can eat!"

"All right, all right, keep your fur on," Lusa said with a sigh. She slowly got to her paws and stumbled outside, followed by Ujurak and Toklo. "Brown bears," Lusa whispered to Kallik, shaking her head. "Remind me why we tried so hard to find them again?"

Kallik woofed with amusement. "Don't worry about Toklo," she said. "I'll find us a seal today. I know I will!"

She could smell the scent that she'd been following last night; it seemed much closer now that the storm had passed and the air was clear. Keeping an eye on the spirit-bubbles under her paws, Kallik led the way across the snow. They'd been walking only for a short while when she spotted what she was looking for—a hole in the ice. "Look," she hissed.

"What is it?" Toklo asked.

"A seal hole. Wait here."

The others sat down and watched her creep across the ice, putting one paw quietly in front of the next. She remembered watching her mother sneak up on a seal's breathing hole like this. Nisa had looked so sure, so confident. Kallik hoped she looked that way to her friends, too.

She settled down next to the hole, rested her nose on her paws, and stared intently. She'd need to move as fast as lightning once a seal's head popped out. It meant focusing all her attention on the hole and not moving a muscle, no matter how long she had to wait. Even the tiniest twitch would warn the seal that she was there. She couldn't just crouch on the ice; she had to be *part* of the ice.

The wind drifted softly across her back, scattering small showers of snow into the air. Kallik stared into the circle of dark water, still and deep and black like the night sky when it was full of clouds and the ice spirits were hidden. One of her paws itched, but she forced herself to keep still.

She could feel the weight of the other three bears behind her, waiting expectantly. Every time one of them shifted, Kallik felt it like a tremor in the ice. Their restlessness was like ants crawling over her pelt. Didn't they understand how long this could take? They couldn't stalk the seal like a hare or a ground squirrel; they had to wait for the seal to come to them.

"Maybe you should stick your paw in there and see if you can feel anything," Toklo called. His claws scraped against the ice with a loud squeak.

"*Shhh!*" Kallik whispered, frustrated. "You'll scare it away. Stay still!"

"It just seems like this is taking a really long time," he grumbled.

"Stop fidgeting," she hissed. "You're distracting me."

"Oh, I'm sorry," Toklo muttered, just loud enough for her to hear. "I didn't mean to *distract* you from the *fascinating* water you were staring at. I'm sure lying still and doing nothing is very *difficult* and important."

"Toklo, *shhhhh*." Kallik was grateful for the sound of Ujurak shushing Toklo. It was impossible for her to focus with Toklo wriggling around and making annoying comments all the time.

She took a deep breath and tried to think of nothing except the jagged hole in the ice in front of her. Seals . . . warm meat crunching under her teeth . . .

"HHRRFFFF," Toklo huffed behind her. Kallik's concentration was broken. She nearly spun around to growl at him, but just then a flash of brown fur appeared in the hole. A seal!

Kallik lunged forward, her claws outstretched, but they closed on empty air. She hadn't been quick enough! A flipper smacked her paws, and then the seal splashed down into the water again and disappeared.

Frustration surged through her.

"Look what you did!" she snarled, spinning on Toklo.

"What *I* did?" he barked. "*You're* the one who was too slow!"

"You distracted me!" she growled, pacing toward him. "Now that seal won't be back for ages!"

"You said the ice was your home and you knew how to hunt out here. But clearly you don't! You can't hunt at all!"

"Not with you whining and fidgeting and scaring off all the prey, I can't!" Kallik roared.

"Prey!" Toklo scoffed. "There's hardly anything out here. We can't survive by eating snow, can we? You obviously can't provide for us the way I fed all of us on the land."

Kallik wanted to claw the smug look right off his face. She paced forward until she was nose to nose with Toklo, and the two bears glared furiously at each other. She lifted her head. She was bigger than Toklo now, although he was broader across his shoulders. She was sure she could take him in a fight.

Maybe that was what he needed. Maybe someone had to batter some sense into his thick skull so he'd stop griping and complaining and finally accept that this was her world and she knew what she was doing.

She growled deep in her throat, and so did Toklo. Her claws sank into the snow, ready for action. If he wanted a fight, she was ready to give him one.

CHAPTER FOUR

Toklo

"*How dare you blame this on* me?" Toklo growled. He could smell Kallik's warm breath barely a muzzlelength from his nose. Her black eyes glittered with fury. "It's *your* fault we have nothing to eat right now, not mine!"

He bunched his muscles to spring. If she attacked him, he'd fight back. At least that would take his mind off his growling, empty stomach. He opened and closed his jaws, baring his sharp teeth. Kallik should watch who she messed with!

"Toklo, calm down." Ujurak swiped at the snow between them, forcing Toklo to take a step back. He sounded just like Oka when she'd scold Tobi and Toklo for bickering over newkill. "Kallik knows what she's doing."

"Oh, really? It doesn't seem like it!" Toklo snarled.

"Kallik is in charge out here," Ujurak said. "Not you." He dipped his head toward the white bear. "We should all listen to her."

Toklo took another step back, but his hackles were still raised. "I didn't start it! She did!"

"You were like a seal-brained cub, whining and scaring away the prey!" Kallik retorted.

Toklo built himself up to roar at her, but Ujurak slapped his paw down on the ice. "That's enough! If we can't catch a seal here, then we just keep going." He turned his back on them and started off across the ice. "Come on, Lusa."

Kallik let out a snort, gave Toklo a disgusted look, and padded after Ujurak. Lusa shook her head vigorously as if she'd been drifting off to sleep and jumped to her paws. She nudged Toklo's flank with her nose. "It'll be all right," she said. "You'll feel better when we catch some prey."

"*If* we catch some prey," Toklo muttered.

Kallik swung her head around and glared at him. "Why don't you do it, then, if you think you're so clever?"

"Maybe I will!" Toklo shot back.

Kallik turned her back on him, sticking her nose in the air.

Toklo looked down at the bubbles in the ice and growled deep in his throat. He didn't see any spirits there, just unhelpful shadows. Those weren't going to give him any clues. He started to trot, staying on the snow so he wouldn't slip on the ice and covering the ground with long strides until he was galloping. He ran right past Kallik and Ujurak, but they didn't say anything about him taking the lead. Huh! Probably because they had no idea where they were going.

A tremor of unease ran through him. How could he hunt out here? The ice told him nothing. On land, he could find pawprints on the ground or the marks of something passing through the bushes, crushing leaves and snapping twigs, so he could follow his prey and catch it. But how would he know where the seals were hiding out here?

His long brown pelt billowed around him as he ran. For a moment he felt powerful again. White bears didn't scare him. Even on the ice, he was still a strong, dangerous bear! He opened his mouth and roared. The sound echoed across the snow as if it could be heard skylengths and skylengths away.

Underneath his paws, the ice creaked, and he thought he felt a shudder in the slippery surface. Even the ice was scared of him! Ha! Now all he needed was a seal, and then the other bears would start listening to him again.

Suddenly he lifted his head and sniffed. That scent . . . it was like the smell Kallik had followed to the last hole. Was it the smell of seal? Only one way to find out. Toklo picked up speed, following the scent until he saw a dark circle in the ice. It was another seal's breathing hole, standing out like Kallik's black nose against her white fur.

Toklo glanced over his shoulder. The others were several bearlengths away. Maybe he could catch a seal before they caught up! That would show Kallik! She was too slow, but he wouldn't be. He crouched down beside the hole, just as she had done. The smell of prey was so strong, his stomach spasmed painfully. His ears twitched as he stared at the hole. Where was that stupid seal?

He saw a flash of movement below the water as a dark shape shot past the hole without popping up. Maybe it was like the salmon in the river; if the seal didn't stop for him, he just had to be faster! Toklo plunged his front paw into the water.

A jolt shot up his leg. The water was *freezing*! He felt a slick body whisk past his paw, but he couldn't get a grip on anything. Frustrated, he pulled back, shaking his wet paw. It felt like icicles were starting to crisp on his fur.

He'd been so close! Now he could see dark shapes moving under the bubble-filled ice, as if the seals were swimming around right below him, laughing at him. Why did he have to wait for them to surface? Sitting by a hole was a stupid way to hunt. He just needed to make more holes and go in after the seals, instead of waiting for them to come to him! That wasn't how a real bear hunted!

Toklo jumped at the edge of the hole with his paws stretched out, trying to break off some of the ice to make the hole bigger. If it were more like a river, he'd be able to seize a seal just like a fish and drag it right out. He pictured the look on Kallik's face when she realized he was a better hunter than her, even out here in her own territory!

Ice shattered under his paws, sending splinters into the air that caught the sunlight in bright dazzles as they fell.

"Stop!" Kallik yelled. "You'll frighten the seals away! Stop!"

But Toklo kept pounding, rearing up on his hind legs and bringing his front paws crashing down again and again. He knew this would work! It had to! He was so hungry and so frustrated and so ready to tear something apart. Something splashed bright red against the snow, and he realized he'd cut his pads on a splinter of ice. It didn't matter; he couldn't feel them anyway. His paws were too numb with the cold, especially the one he'd dipped in the water.

"Toklo, please stop!" Lusa barked. "You're hurting yourself!"

Toklo stood for a moment with all four feet on the ice, breathing hard. The jagged hole in front of him was bigger, but empty of seals. Spots of red splattered the snow around the edges. He growled and stomped away from the hole. He could hear more ice splinters crunching under his paws, although he still couldn't feel them.

"Toklo, wait!" he heard. It was Kallik calling to him. "Don't go that way!"

Now she was trying to boss him around. She just didn't want him to take the lead! Perhaps she could tell that he was closer to catching a seal than she had been. Toklo started running, letting the wind carry away the voices calling behind him. There had to be another seal hole out here somewhere. He swung his head from side to side, scanning the ice and sniffing. The scent of prey was muddled by the sharp smell of his own blood coming from his paws.

Toklo slipped on a patch of bare ice and skidded several bearlengths before he was able to get his paws under him and scramble up again. He glared down at the ice and noticed that it looked darker than the ice they'd been on before. Large bubbles surged and wandered just below the surface. It was almost as if he could see right through to the dark, cold sea underneath.

If the ice was thinner here, surely he could find another seal

hole? He started running again, avoiding the slicker patches
of ice. Snow crunched under his paws. He saw a dark spot up
ahead and leaped toward it.

Suddenly, Toklo skidded as a slab of ice tilted underneath
him. Cold seawater bubbled up from a jagged line just in front
of his paws. There was a crack in the ice! He scrabbled with
his paws as he slid toward it and managed to leap over the
crack at the last moment.

As he landed, the ice on the other side wobbled dangerously, and bubbling water flooded over his paws. Toklo dug
in his claws to steady himself. His heart was pounding. This
whole place felt so wrong. Why would any bears live with only
a thin, bubble-filled sheet of stuff that could melt between
their paws and the yawning, hungry ocean at any moment?

He looked around and saw his friends padding cautiously
toward him. Lusa's steps were tentative, as if she was testing
every movement before putting her weight down. Kallik's
paws padded expertly over the surface, gliding so that she
hardly lifted each foot up before moving it forward. Behind
her, Ujurak was standing up on his hind legs so he could watch
Toklo.

"Be careful, Toklo!" Kallik called. Her voice didn't sound
bossy to him anymore. It sounded . . . worried. "There's something wrong with the ice." She lowered her head to stare into
the bubbles. "It's—I don't understand—but I think it's not as
thick as it should be. It's not as thick as the ice where I was
born."

"Listen to Kallik, Toklo!" Ujurak cried. "She knows what

she's talking about!"

"Oh, Toklo!" Lusa yelped. "Please come back!"

Toklo took a step toward them, trying to go around the crack through which seawater was still bubbling. To his horror, he heard a loud *SNAP!* The world tilted crazily around him, and before he could scrabble backward, the ice rolled away from his paws and sent him plunging into the freezing water.

All the air was knocked out of Toklo's chest by the impact with the water and the shock of how cold it was. The sea closed over his head, surrounding him in darkness and eerie silence. It was still and heavy and bottomless—nothing like a river or even the lake. And there were no brown bear spirits here to help him. *Oka! Tobi!* But all he could hear were the weird creaks and groans of the ice overhead.

Desperately Toklo hauled his way back up to the surface. He knew he couldn't take a breath until his head was above water. But instead of breaking through into fresh air, Toklo felt his head bump against a roof of solid ice. A swell of water tugged at his fur, dragging him away from the hole he'd fallen through. He flailed his paws, trying to get back to it, but he didn't even know where it was anymore. The surface was too churned up with bubbles and splinters of ice to show where the crack had appeared.

He was trapped!

Toklo tried clawing at the ice above his head, pushing against it, scrabbling at its underneath until his claws were nearly wrenched out of his pads, but it was as solid as rock.

The glare of daylight beyond it tortured him with the promise of air he couldn't get to. Where was the hole? The saltwater stung his eyes so he could barely see to look for it. He felt panic rising as his chest began to ache. His vision was getting red around the edges.

He was going to drown, just as he'd always feared, but it wouldn't be in a river or a lake with the spirits of his mother and brother—it would be here, in this horrible, cold, empty place.

Tobi, he called in his mind as everything started to go dark. *Oka . . . please help me. . . .*

But how could they help him? The only spirits here were the white bears in the ice, and they were the ones trapping him down here. They wanted him to drown.

Nothing was going to save him now.

CHAPTER FIVE

Ujurak

As Toklo vanished into the dark water, Ujurak felt a tremor ripple through his body. He didn't stop to think about what he was doing. He was already running toward the hole in the ice as his body began to change shape.

He could hear Kallik shouting, "No! Ujurak! It's not safe!" but his ears were pulling back into his head, and he barely registered her words.

His thick brown fur shrank and melted away into a thick, rubbery white skin. His forehead bulged out and up. His whole body got bigger and fatter, surging out like a bubble expanding. As he dove toward the hole, his paws shrank into flat white flippers and his back legs joined together into one long tail.

The cold sea closed over him with a splash, but his new layers of fat and blubber kept him warm. He beat his tail and small, square flippers to propel himself forward, underneath the clear roof of gleaming ice.

What am I? He spun in a slow circle, studying his sleek,

pale body. He felt the water ripple around him in a comforting, supportive way. He knew just how to move, how to send himself in a new direction with the smallest twitch of his flippers.

Whale. Beluga whale. Of course.

It was strangely beautiful down here, with beams of sunlight filtering through the ice and disappearing into the darkness far below. For a moment, Ujurak floated in place, mesmerized by the light. He drifted slowly, making a high twittering sound as he gazed around at the ocean.

A peculiar shape caught his attention. What was *that*? Something big and much too furry for the ocean. That wasn't supposed to be here. It seemed to know that, too; it was pounding at the ice above it in a frantic way, but its motions were getting weaker and weaker.

Curious, Ujurak swam a little closer. It was a bear! And not even a white bear; this one was *brown*! What was a brown—

His tiny whale eyes blinked as he remembered. Shifting into other animals was getting dangerous. He kept coming so close to forgetting who he really was: a brown bear, with bear friends who needed him.

Ujurak gave a powerful flick of his tail and surged toward Toklo. He charged into the bear cub with surprising force, shoving Toklo toward the hole he'd fallen through. Toklo flailed his paws in a panic, perhaps thinking he was being attacked by an orca, but Ujurak swung his hefty body—nimble and weightless in the water—and avoided his claws.

The ice made a loud cracking sound as Toklo's back hit the

spot where it had split in two. His head popped out through the hole into the air and he threw his front paws onto the ice shelf, hanging on desperately. Ujurak used his wide, blunt nose to shove Toklo again from below, pushing him up onto the unbroken ice closer to Kallik and Lusa. Toklo dug his claws in and pulled himself away from the hole, collapsing onto the ice and retching seawater.

Ujurak waited for a moment to be sure that Toklo was breathing, then he shot a stream of water out of his blowhole and let himself drift back down into the water. Through the fragile sheet of ice, he could see Kallik and Lusa racing toward Toklo, calling his name. Their voices were muffled, but he could still hear their alarm.

Foolish Toklo, running out onto the thin ice like that. He should have waited for Kallik! Couldn't he understand that they all depended on the white bear out here? Ujurak should have guessed that it would be hard on Toklo, giving up his leadership. Toklo was used to being the one who took care of them all, and he'd done it well . . . but why did he have to be so stubborn about everything?

It made Ujurak tired just thinking about the fight Toklo and Kallik had nearly had, or the arguments that probably still lay ahead as Toklo tried to adjust to letting someone else lead and hunt for him.

But under the ice, it was quiet and peaceful. Kallik had promised there would be plenty of prey to fish from the water, but right now it seemed as if he were the only creature alive in the whole ocean. If he tried looking with his eyes, the dark water around him seemed empty, shimmering blue and green in the rays of sunlight through the ice.

But when he used his whale senses he could detect movement and life in every direction. The twittering sound he made brought pictures back to him somehow, as though it was echoing off the faraway shapes and turning them into images in his head. For a start, he knew that there were seals everywhere, swimming and playing and chasing fish.

Curious, he swam toward the closest group and watched them hunt for a while. Like sleek, silent wolves they circled a ball of fish that swerved and darted and folded over itself like a single dazzling wing of black and silver. At an invisible signal, the seals closed in, jaws snapping at mouthfuls of sparkling fish. They were so fast, so strong as they pushed through the water, that it seemed impossible for the silver wing to survive; it shattered like ice, then re-formed a heartbeat later and pulsed into the darker water, out of sight.

Ujurak's mind felt fuzzy, as if he'd forgotten something, but he was too distracted by the beauty of the undersea world to focus on remembering. He swam on, noticing how the light around him grew dimmer and brighter like sunlight striking through trees. He guessed it depended on how thick the ice was over his head. Where the water was filled with pale light, the ice must be dangerously thin. He wondered how thick the ice had been before. A flickering hole of bright white caught his eye. A seal's breathing hole was directly above him. Ujurak swam toward it, wondering if he could learn anything about hunting by seeing the hole from the other side.

A large dark shadow lay unmoving on the ice beside the hole. It took Ujurak a moment to realize it was a full-grown white bear waiting for a seal to surface. Ujurak considered popping up and giving the bear a shock: a huge white whale instead of the seal it was waiting for! But then Ujurak thought how sharp the bear's claws must be, and how it would probably be just as happy to eat a whale as a seal, and he quickly turned to swim away.

Gigantic pale bulks appeared out of the shadows ahead, hanging in the water like smooth-edged clouds. With a start, Ujurak realized they were beluga whales like him. He slowed down, not wanting to provoke a conflict. But the whales just blinked at him as he approached, twitching their flippers to stay in line with the current.

One of them opened its huge mouth, letting out a stream of bubbles. "Seen any prey?" he asked in a series of clicks and squeals.

"Sorry, no," Ujurak replied, flicking his tail to propel himself past. He couldn't exactly remember what he'd been doing a few moments ago, but he felt hungry, so he assumed he hadn't found anything to eat. The other whales bobbed slightly in the wave he'd created below the surface. Part of him wanted to stop and talk, but he was running out of air and needed to find somewhere to breathe . . . preferably somewhere without a white bear waiting for prey!

His squeaks bounced off the ice overhead and told him there was a patch of open water nearby. Ujurak twitched his flippers and angled up toward it, feeling the water whirl past him as he swam to the surface. He nudged his way into the air and inhaled through his blowhole, blinking at the glaring whiteness of the ice. The patch of open water he'd found was small, no longer than two of him, but it was enough to give him room to breathe for a moment. Jagged pieces of broken ice around the hole hinted that something had smashed its way up from below.

He blew out a spurt of water and inhaled again, preparing to dive. His stomach was demanding food, and something told him he could find it on the ocean floor. With a flip of his tail, he dove into the water and spiraled into the depths.

He still felt as if he was missing something—as if he'd been in the middle of something and had forgotten to go back and finish it. Or as if he'd left something important behind. But he had no idea what it could be. The blue shadows turned black the farther down he swam, and sometimes he could rely only on his squeaks bouncing clearly back to tell him there were no obstacles in his way, since he couldn't see anything with his eyes in the pitch darkness. Swerving up to a lighter patch of water, he found a shallower area where a sandy shelf was just visible below him.

Ujurak sucked seawater into his mouth and puffed a strong jet of water at the sandy bottom. Sand flew up in a whoosh, clouding the water around him, but he could see crabs and shrimp that he'd dislodged from the seafloor scrambling for cover. Feeling a thrill of satisfaction, he gobbled up as many as he could fit into his mouth in one swoop, swallowing them whole.

This kind of hunting was fun! Easier than chasing after fast, wriggly little fish like the seals had to. Ujurak swam a little farther and did it again, blasting more crustaceans out of the sand and bolting them down.

When his belly felt full, he flicked his tail and rose to the surface again for air. He felt quite pleased with himself, but there was also a sense of unease prickling along his skin. Something was wrong. Something was *missing*. He wasn't supposed to be alone. Where was his pod? Shouldn't he be traveling with other whales? How had he lost them?

He searched his memory, trying to remember who he'd been with, but he couldn't recall any other whales. That was strange. He knew he should be surrounded by others; he had a definite memory of warmth and friendship, but he couldn't attach any faces to it. He floated in the open water for a moment, breathing in and out, and then dove back down. Perhaps if he kept swimming around, he'd find his pod around here somewhere. They couldn't have gone far.

As he paddled swiftly along under the ice, the sound-pictures in his mind told him that there was something large up ahead—much, much larger than a whale. He couldn't imagine a creature that big, but it was moving, so it must be alive. It seemed to be making odd pinging and creaking and humming noises. Ujurak swam toward it, sending out squeaks to find out more.

The closer he got, the more he was aware of a noisy thrumming vibrating through the water. It stung against his skin and made his head ache. Tense with alarm, Ujurak was about to turn back, when a vast gray shape loomed out of the water, charging straight toward him.

It was an underwater firebeast! It had the smell of firebeasts and the fierce glow of their eyes and the same hard shiny skin, but it was long and sleek like a fish without flippers or paws. A short, spiky tail spun at the back to keep it moving forward, thrusting it through the water much faster than Ujurak could swim. Hurling himself sideways, he bounced through a storm of bubbles as he veered out of the way just before it sliced through the water where he had been swimming.

The rush of water as it went past tossed Ujurak over and over, leaving him disoriented and confused. He flailed his huge body as hard as he could, trying to swim away from the rotating tail before it caught him and churned him into pieces. Finally the firebeast disappeared into the dark, leaving a gritty, foamy wake that lashed against Ujurak's skin and tasted like oil.

Stunned, Ujurak drifted for a moment. Had that firebeast taken him on in a fight, and won? Or had it not even noticed that he was there? Whatever that monster was, it would have killed him without a sideways glance—not for prey, not for territory, but purely by accident, because he was in its way.

Even far below the ice, there was death and danger pulsing in the shadows, tasting of oil and flat-faces, and churning animals and fish out of the way as easily as Ujurak had snorted the tiny crabs out of the sand. Ujurak thought he would never feel safe again.

CHAPTER SIX

Kallik

Kallik and Lusa buried their noses in Toklo's freezing wet fur. Long shadows like flat spiky trees stretched over the ice and the blue-gray mounds of snow around them. Darkness was falling, Ujurak was still gone, and Toklo had been lying unconscious since he'd been shoved out of the water by Ujurak's gigantic white flippers.

Kallik rubbed Toklo's back and sides with her paws, trying to warm him up. Snow was melting into her belly fur and she could feel the bone-chilling cold of the ice shelf underneath the snow creeping up through her paws. On the other side of Toklo, Lusa was shivering; Kallik could feel the tremors through Toklo's fur.

"What did Ujurak turn into?" Lusa whispered to Kallik over Toklo's back. "I've never seen a fish that big before."

"That was a kind of whale," Kallik said, remembering the belugas she had played with a long time ago, back when she first left the ice to search for her brother. "I met some while I was traveling by myself. They were friendlier than I thought they would be. I guess they don't eat bears." She looked at the dark hole in the ice where Ujurak had disappeared. He'd been gone for a terribly long time. "Why hasn't he come back yet?"

"I don't know." Lusa licked Toklo's ear. "I hope he comes back soon. I don't know what we're supposed to do now."

Kallik lifted her head and looked up at the deep purple-blue sky, where a few small stars were already twinkling. Even though she was worried about Ujurak, she felt comforted by the sight of the ice spirits watching over them. "We'll wait for him," she said. "He's always come back before."

"Unless he was in trouble," Lusa reminded her. "What if he's hurt? How long should we wait?"

Toklo made a guttural sound deep in his throat and Kallik jumped, startled. Lusa snuggled in as close to him as she could. "Toklo?" she whispered in his ear. "Are you all right?"

Toklo let out a harsh cough that racked his whole body. Over and over he rasped, spitting up saltwater and a strand of damp green weed. Finally he stopped and turned his head toward Lusa. In a low growl, he muttered, "I'm fine."

A rush of relief washed over Kallik. She should never have quarreled with Toklo like that, taunting him into trying to prove that he could hunt here on his own. That wasn't taking care of him; that was putting him in greater danger than starvation or the cold.

"I just lost my footing," Toklo went on gruffly. "Stupid ice. This is no place for brown bears." He gave her a fierce look. "Or black bears, for that matter."

"There are dangerous parts of the ice," Kallik agreed. "You

have to learn to watch for them." She wanted to go on and scold him for not listening to her, for rushing ahead without waiting for her to tell him which way was safe, but she held her tongue, unwilling to start that fight again.

"I guess so," Toklo muttered. "Maybe there's some stuff I still have to learn."

Kallik figured that was as close to an apology as she'd ever get. She ducked her head, acknowledging it.

"I thought you were gone forever," Lusa whimpered, nudging her nose under his chin. "When you vanished under the ice I didn't know how we'd ever find you or get you back, but then Ujurak changed into something—Kallik called it a whale, but it looked like a really, *really* big fish—and he pushed you out and then all we saw was this huge white tail flipping up and then he swam back down and he still hasn't come back, but oh, I'm so glad you're all right!"

Toklo squinted at the crack in the ice, then pushed himself a little farther away from it, as if it might stretch of its own accord and suck him back in.

"Don't worry, Ujurak will come back," Kallik reassured them.

"He'd better!" Toklo snapped. "He made us come on this squirrel-brained mission into the world's most horrible place—if he leaves us here without a word, I swear I will eat him when I find him, no matter how big a fish he is!"

Kallik swallowed her anger at his description of her home. She could hear the worry in his voice, and she knew he was as anxious about Ujurak as she was.

"What do we do if he doesn't come back?" Lusa asked in a small voice. "I mean—we have no idea where to go without him, or how to save the wild."

They were all silent for a moment.

"We'd have to go back to the land," Toklo said at last. "You and me, I mean, Lusa. It wouldn't make sense for us to stay out here without Ujurak."

Lusa gave Kallik a nervous look. "I know you can take care of us, Kallik, but . . . I think Toklo might be right."

Kallik scraped her front paw across the snow. "Right. I know. There's no quest without Ujurak." She leaned over and nuzzled Lusa's tufty ear. "But I would miss you."

"I'd miss you, too," Lusa agreed. "You'd probably be better off without us, though."

I'd certainly be less worried, Kallik thought. "It doesn't matter," she said. "Ujurak will be back. I'm sure of it. And in the meantime, he said I'm supposed to lead us out here. So I think we should do what we did last night—find somewhere to sleep where we'll be safe and warm."

"What if Ujurak comes back looking for us?" Toklo asked, glancing at the open water with a shudder.

"There's enough snow over there for me to make a cave," Kallik said, pointing with her nose. "It's close enough that we'll see him. Come on, we'll feel better when we're warm."

Toklo pushed himself to his paws and winced. He picked up each of his front paws and licked them gingerly. Kallik noticed cuts on his pads, and she remembered the blood on the ice where Toklo had tried to pound his way through to reach the seals. She hoped that it wouldn't attract unwanted attention from full-grown white bears—they'd be able to smell his blood from skylengths away.

"Will you be able to walk?" Lusa asked.

"Of course I will!" Toklo said irritably. "I can't even feel my paws, let alone these tiny little scratches." He hunched his shoulders as Kallik took the lead.

After a moment, she heard him mutter to Lusa, "I will catch a seal next time, you know. I almost had it."

"I don't care *who* catches a seal," Lusa replied in a low voice, "as long as *someone* does . . . and *soon!*"

Guilt flooded through Kallik again. What kind of white bear couldn't even catch a seal? Maybe she couldn't take care of her friends after all. At the same time, she felt a flash of irritation with both Toklo and Lusa. They just needed to give her a chance! She'd followed them trustingly enough on land, even when Toklo failed to catch the prey he went after. He wasn't exactly perfect, either!

She tried to remember how she'd felt among the trees and the grasslands at first—hot, dirty, out of place, and uncomfortable. That must be how they were feeling now. She knew Lusa must miss trees, which made Kallik feel trapped and weighted to the ground. She felt freer here, where she could run in any direction with nothing to block her way . . . but Lusa and Toklo must feel as exposed as a snail on a rock, with nowhere to escape to. It was no wonder they felt so confused and lost.

As she dug into the snow with her paws, Kallik glanced at

the endless horizon and felt comfort in how much wide space there was. The moon was rising, glittering off the ice. They bounced the silvery glow between them, from the sky to the frozen ocean and back again. Moonlight shimmered on the hillocks of snow around them and sparkled on the broken ice where Ujurak had disappeared. Toklo and Lusa had had their time of feeling at home while they'd traveled on land. It was Kallik's turn now.

She stepped back from the cave she'd dug, feeling satisfied. At least that was one thing she could do right. Toklo scrambled inside with a grunt that she decided to accept as a thank-you.

"Go on in and rest," Kallik said, nudging Lusa's side. "You look worn out."

"I feel worn out," Lusa mumbled. Kallik peered at her. Lusa really looked more tired than Kallik had ever seen her, but they hadn't even traveled very far that day. Was she all right? Was she getting sick?

Lusa saw the look on Kallik's face and poked her with her nose. "Don't worry, Kallik, we'll be all right. We're just getting used to the ice, that's all."

"Sure," Kallik said, ducking her head.

"And look!" Lusa barked, spotting the colorful lights in the sky over Kallik's shoulder. "The bear spirits! See, Kallik? They're watching us—they want us to be here."

The two bears leaned against each other for a moment, watching the green and gold lights dance around one another, flaring brilliantly across the darkness. But Kallik's fur prickled. The lights were paler tonight, the colors more dim. Did that mean they were farther away? Were the spirits leaving them?

Maybe they're just sleeping, she told herself, and yawned hugely. Maybe once she'd slept for a while, too, then everything would seem better.

CHAPTER SEVEN

Ujurak

"Pukak!" a bubbling voice called. "Pukak! Is that you?"

Ujurak twisted around in the water. His head still throbbed from his encounter with the firebeast, so it took him a moment to focus on the female beluga whale who was swimming up to him. She didn't look familiar, but her eyes shone with hope. She nudged him away from the churned-up path of the firebeast, into calmer waters. The sound of its thrumming was fading away, but the ocean still stank of oil and prickled with heat that didn't belong there.

"Pukak?" the whale asked again, swimming around him.

"No, I'm sorry," Ujurak said, realizing that she was saying a name. "I am called Ujurak."

"Oh," she said, drifting a short distance away from him. "Well. Don't you know you shouldn't be here? This is where they always come."

"Who?"

"Who?" she snorted. "The poisonbeasts! This is their territory. Everybody knows that."

Ujurak blinked, puzzled. "You mean—" He tried to say "firebeast," and then realized there was no word for "fire" in his language. He could sense the word in his head, but he couldn't say it out loud. *So how do I know it at all?* He was a whale, wasn't he? "Poisonbeast," he said instead. "That giant thing that just went by?"

The beluga stared at him. "You really don't know about them? You must come from very far away." She blew out a stream of bubbles. "I wouldn't mind living where there aren't any poisonbeasts. Anyway, just be more careful from now on." She turned and started to swim away.

"Wait!" Ujurak called. "I want to know more about them!" He hurried after her, flicking his long tail. "Are there lots of poisonbeasts down here?" he puffed as he caught up to her.

"Too many," she said bitterly.

Ujurak's squeaks bounced off something large to their left. He turned his head, trying to figure out what it was. It wasn't moving, so it couldn't be a poisonbeast, but it was just as large—perhaps even larger.

"What is that?" he asked the female whale. He didn't want to swim any closer to it; he'd learned his lesson with the poisonbeast, but he could sense it looming in the distance. Something vast and ominous, humming with the same terrible vibrations as the poisonbeast.

The whale shuddered. "We don't know what to call it. It's a giant, rock-eating beast that burrows into the ocean floor and makes all the water around it sick. It stands on four giant legs and we stay as far away from it as we can."

A small school of fish swam slowly past, their silver scales dull in the smoky water. The female whale waved them away from Ujurak with her tail. "Don't eat those," she warned, although he hadn't been planning to. "All the fish around here will make you sick if you eat them."

"I feel dizzy," Ujurak wheezed. "The poison—"

She peered at him closely. "You probably just need air. How long has it been since you breathed?"

He realized she was right and felt foolish. The poisonbeast had frightened him so much, he'd forgotten about needing to surface to breathe.

"Come on," she said, swimming up toward the light that shone dimly far over their heads. Ujurak followed her, happy to leave the poisoned water and distant thrumming.

"Uglu! Uglu!" Ujurak heard clicking and squeaking up ahead. It sounded like a crowd of beluga whales, all of them calling the same name. "Uglu!"

The female put on a burst of speed and led him up through the water, breaking the surface at a breathing hole in the ice. This one was much larger than the holes the seals used, and there was a whole pod of whales resting in it. Endless stretches of ice glittered around the hole, curving into tall frozen shapes and covered in a light dusting of snow. The sparkly, hard-edged, nearly blue whiteness was striking against the soft, squeaky, gray whiteness of the whales.

Ujurak blew out a spout of water and took a breath of cold air. He saw an old, painfully thin whale flopped halfway onto a floating chunk of ice, basking in the last rays of the sunset, and he realized that it was nearly nightfall. The silvery moon was already sneaking over the edge of the sky. He had a strange feeling he was supposed to be somewhere, but he couldn't remember where.

"He was all alone!" his new friend was telling the other whales in squeaks and whistles. "The poisonbeast was about to attack him! But I saved him. He didn't even know about them."

"Wow," said one of the younger whales. "You're a hero, Uglu!"

Uglu flicked her tail. "I'd better get back down there. Pukak might need my help, too." She took a deep breath, nodded good-bye to Ujurak, and dove back into the ocean.

Ujurak saw a pair of older whales exchange mournful glances. Several whales crowded around him, clicking and whistling curiously. Three young whales that had been spitting water at one another stopped playing and hurried over to prod and peer at him. He was surprised to find he liked their playful poking; it felt friendly and comforting instead of intrusive.

"Were you really that close to a poisonbeast?" one of them asked. "Wasn't it so scary?"

"Oh, yes," Ujurak replied. "They're horrible."

"Where are you from?" a male beluga squeaked nosily. "What's the hunting like where you've been swimming?"

"Where's the rest of your pod?" a young female chimed in.

"I . . . I'm not sure," Ujurak stammered, trying to think. He couldn't remember anything before the poisonbeast. Would the whales believe him if he told them that?

"I've come a long way," he said finally. "I let a current bring me here, because the hunting was not so great where I was . . . uh, before."

"Well, it's not much better here!" said the same male. "You'd probably be better off going back there!"

"Oh, don't be rude," said one of the older whales, nudging the young male aside. "Let the poor thing rest. You can pester him with your questions later, if he'll let you."

"Whatever," said the young beluga, splashing Ujurak with his tail as he swam away. The others drifted away as well, whispering to one another and peeking at him curiously over their tails.

"Don't mind the young 'uns," said the old whale. "Their world is different from the one I grew up in. I'm Kassuk, by the way."

"I'm Ujurak," answered Ujurak, grateful to be spared any more awkward questions. "Why did Uglu leave so quickly?"

Kassuk sighed. "Poor Uglu. She lost her calf, Pukak, not very long ago. He went out hunting and never came back, and now she goes out every day searching for him." The old whale stirred the water with one of his flippers, looking sad. "We all know he must be dead by now. A young whale like him would never have survived on his own. He probably strayed too far into poisonbeast territory and one of them killed him. But Uglu won't accept it. She doesn't even hear us when we try to talk to her about it. She just keeps searching."

"Pukak," Ujurak echoed. "That's what she called me when

she first saw me." He was hit by a wave of grief for the mother endlessly searching for her lost calf.

"She'll be back soon to sleep," Kassuk assured him. "You can stay with us for the night if you want, and search for your own pod in the morning. Or if you need to, you can stay with us. You don't look like you'd cause much trouble." He flicked a small spray of water at Ujurak in a friendly way.

"Thank you," Ujurak said. "I'd appreciate that." He didn't know where else he could go to sleep, and he felt safe here, surrounded by so many other whales.

In the glow of the moonlight, Ujurak saw Uglu come swimming up from the depths to join them. Her small round eyes were unreadable in the silvery light; she didn't look as if she'd found anything to give her hope, but she didn't look grief-stricken, either. Did she really believe her calf was still alive, somewhere in the distant black water?

The pod gathered into a close knot, huddled together on the surface of the water. Soon most of the whales were asleep. Ujurak stayed awake for a while longer, trying to pull something from his memory. The poisonbeast and the rock-eating creature had frightened him, but he felt as if there was something more he knew about them, if he could only dig it out of his mind.

Before he could, however, he felt his thoughts drift into calmness with the lapping waves, and soon he was asleep, too.

The next morning, Kassuk and a few of the young whales took Ujurak hunting with them. He felt bubbles of joy rising in his chest as he helped them herd schools of silvery fish together. When there were so many fish trapped in one place by the other whales, it was easy to swoop in and catch at least a few of them in his mouth. Still, he could see why the pod was worried. It was difficult to find a school with enough fish for all of them, and several had that dull, sickly sheen he'd noticed in the ones near the rock-eating beast.

He asked Kassuk about it once they were back at the breathing hole, letting the early slanting sun soak into their pale skin. "Is it this hard to hunt everywhere?"

Kassuk sighed. "It is now. It wasn't like this when I was a calf. You couldn't move for fish then. Some of the whales think we will run out of food altogether soon. There's a sickness in the water, thanks to the landwalkers."

"No!" Ujurak cried, starting to panic. He twisted his body, sending a wave of water cascading onto the ice beside them. "There must be something we can do!" *He* had to stop these landwalkers, whatever they were; they had put his friends, his pod, his whole kind in danger! He had to save the water and the whales and everything that lived out here.

But how? There must be a way; he had known about it ever since he first dove into this water—whenever that was. How many seasons had he been here? He shook his head, trying to remember. There was someone to help him . . . wasn't there? He had a feeling that he wasn't alone, but that didn't make sense. There weren't any other belugas with him when the female found him. And even if he did have friends somewhere, what could they do against all the flat-faces and firebeasts and poisonbeasts and oil-sucking things in the world?

Kassuk gave him a confused look. "What do you mean, 'do'?"

"We can't change the tides," put in another whale. "The sickness is like the currents—it just is. Whales will learn to live with it."

"Or die," an old male said gloomily.

But I'm not a whale, Ujurak thought suddenly. A shiver of realization ran through his skin. He wasn't a whale; he hadn't swum here from a far-distant pod. All he could remember was that he should have fur and claws. . . .

I'm a BEAR!

Maybe whales couldn't do anything . . . but maybe bears could.

His flesh prickled as if fur might come bursting out of it at any moment. He needed to be back with his friends. *His friends.* Toklo, Lusa, and Kallik appeared in his mind like a bolt of lightning. He'd forgotten about them again!

"I'm sorry, I have to go," Ujurak said to Kassuk, ducking away. "I left someone—they're waiting for me. I'm sorry." The old whale nodded, looking surprised, and Ujurak dove into the sea again, beating his tail to swim faster.

The dark cold water closed around him, and he tried to think of nothing but bears. *Don't let me forget again. I have to get back to them before I forget . . . while I still know that I'm a bear.* He wished he could swim even faster. How long had he been gone? He couldn't keep changing shape like this. One day he'd forget altogether, and end up trapped in some other animal's body.

I'm a bear! he roared inside his mind. *I won't forget. . . . I won't forget. . . . I won't forget. . . .*

CHAPTER EIGHT

Lusa

"Wake up!"

Lusa covered her nose with her paws and groaned.

"Lusa! Wake up! Come on!" Toklo prodded her again. Through her half-open eyes, Lusa could see light through the walls of the snow cave, so she must have slept through the night. But it didn't feel like long enough. She was still so tired.

"Lusa, please!" Toklo barked. "I've been trying to wake you for *ages*. Ujurak is back!"

"Oh," Lusa said, struggling to open her eyes all the way. She tried to sit up and nearly fell over. Her paws felt like heavy useless fish at the ends of her legs. "Is he all right?"

Just then Ujurak came bundling into the cave with Kallik right behind him, shoving him inside. His fur was soaking wet and he was shivering, and his eyes looked strangely unfocused, as if he were watching something inside himself instead of seeing his friends.

Kallik and Toklo crowded around Ujurak, ushering him

into the center of the cave next to Lusa and curling beside him to warm him up. With a grateful sigh, Lusa lay back down and rested her head on her paws. Even Ujurak's cold, wet side pressed against hers didn't make her feel more awake.

"Where did you go?" Kallik prompted. "You were gone for so long!"

Ujurak stared down at his paws. "I was with a pod of other whales. I mean . . . a pod of whales. Not like me. Not bears." He sounded almost as tired as Lusa felt.

"Did you see any seals down there?" Toklo asked. "Are there any breathing holes close by?"

"What was it like under the ice?" Kallik pressed, her eyes filled with curiosity. "Were you scared? You didn't see any orcas, did you?"

"Did you like being a whale?" Lusa murmured through a yawn.

"It must be great to be able to swim so far," Kallik said wistfully. "And to stay underwater for that long . . . I bet you saw all kinds of things bears never get to see!"

Ujurak shifted on his paws. "I prefer being a bear," he said.

As the others kept pestering him, Lusa let herself start to drift off again. It was so cozy in here . . . so warm, and comfortable, and she was so tired. . . .

"LUSA!" Toklo shouted.

Lusa jumped awake. Her friends were gone, and she was alone in the cave, except for Toklo's grumpy face poking back in through the entrance.

"What is the matter with you?" he growled. "Come on, the sun will wake you up. Get out here."

With a huge sigh, Lusa struggled to her paws and followed him out of the cave. She was surprised at how far up the sun was in the sky—it was at least halfway to its highest point. They must have stayed in the cave to warm Ujurak up for a while, although Lusa had slept through it all. She swung her head around to look for the small brown bear and saw him standing not too far from the crack in the ice. His head was bowed, and for a moment she worried that he might dive back into the dark water.

"He won't say if he saw any seals," Toklo grumbled. "Or if there are any we could hunt around here. Absolutely useless."

"That's all right," Kallik said, sniffing the air. "I smell prey!" She nodded toward the sun.

"Come *on*, Ujurak!" Toklo called. "We're not going to get wherever you want us to go by standing around and staring into the water."

Lusa chuffed with laughter, but Ujurak just blinked, then turned and shambled up beside them. His paws crunched on the ice, and the shadows of the snow piles around them rippled across his brown fur.

"Cheer up, whale-brain," Toklo said, nudging Ujurak's side.

"Whales have perfectly good brains," Ujurak retorted. He shook his head. "I mean, not as good as bear brains, of course."

"Well, of course!" Toklo said. He sprang after Kallik, who

was already trotting up a long snowy slope in the direction of the prey scent. Ujurak and Lusa followed more slowly after them.

The bright sun warmed Lusa's fur and did make her feel a little better, although she could tell that she'd still be able to fall asleep in a heartbeat if she had the chance. Her paws churned through the snow as she tried to keep up with the others. In the lead, Kallik kept padding faster and faster, as if she knew for certain there was something ahead of them. Lusa couldn't smell anything, but she was concentrating too much on staying awake to argue.

Toklo's question echoed in her mind as snow and ice crunched underpaw. Was there something wrong with her? All she wanted to do was curl up somewhere and sleep. She'd never felt like this before, not even when they were travel- ing much farther every day, through the mountains and across vast plains where the grass rippled like water.

She couldn't tell the others. If she was sick, it would ruin their whole quest. But how could she save the wild when she could barely put one paw in front of the other? Lusa gritted her teeth. She would keep going, no matter what. She'd come all this way; she wasn't going to let a little sleepiness stop her now. She'd just keep walking and hope that her friends didn't notice.

Immediately in front of her, Toklo was moving much slower than the day before, checking the ice every few steps to make sure it was firm underneath him. He seemed less interested in taking the lead today, although Lusa was sure that if Kallik didn't find prey soon, that would change.

The sun slid slowly down the sky, casting longer and longer shadows across the snowy landscape. Lusa watched a few clouds amble from one edge of the sky to another. Her paws began to ache, and her eyes itched from the brightness of the sunshine on the snow. They'd been walking for *ages*. Lusa found it hard to imagine that Kallik had really smelled something this far away. Her stomach growled sadly. She'd so wanted her friend to be right this time.

"Here!" Kallik suddenly called from up ahead. "Look what I found!"

Lusa dug her paws in and sprinted over a small hill of snow. She slid down the other side and nearly crashed into Ujurak, who was standing with his head raised, staring at the edge of the sky where bright blue met shimmering white ice.

Next to Kallik's paws was a breathing hole . . . and lying beside it was the half-eaten carcass of a seal!

Lusa gasped. "Kallik, that's amazing!" She turned to look back at where they'd come. The cave where they'd slept was skylengths away now. "How did you smell it from all that way?"

Kallik shrugged and scraped her claws across the ice. "It's a lot easier out here where the ice doesn't muddle up my nose the way earth and trees and plants do," she said.

"That is really impressive," Ujurak said admiringly.

Toklo just grunted. He lowered his head to sniff the carcass, then turned to look around suspiciously. "This smells like another white bear," he said.

"Uh-oh," Lusa said, casting a nervous glance at the hill behind them. "Some bear must have left it here. What if it comes back?"

"Are we invading their territory?" Toklo asked. His brown fur bristled across his back. "Not that I'm afraid of fighting another bear for food! I say it's their loss! It's just . . . uh . . . white bears can get very . . . big."

"There are no territories on the ice," Kallik said, tilting her head at him in a puzzled way. "Everyone takes what food they can get. Sometimes it means frightening away a smaller bear, if that's what you have to do—when I was on the ice with Nisa and Taqqiq, we were scared away from food more than once!"

"Makes sense to me," Toklo agreed. "If a bear was silly enough to leave food out in the open, they'd better expect someone to take it."

Lusa's ears pricked with alarm. She remembered the size of the white bears at Great Bear Lake. One of *those* might come along and chase them off at any moment? She didn't like the sound of that! She was *much* smaller than any of those bears. She'd probably make just as good a meal for one of them as the seal lying on the ice in front of her.

"Well, let's not wait for whoever caught this to come back," Kallik decided. She bent down and tore off a piece of flesh. "Try it!"

They all crouched and began to dig in, although Lusa kept an eye out for angry white bears who might be returning for their prey.

"It's good!" Toklo said, sounding surprised. "Fattier and greasier than a rabbit or a squirrel, but that's all right by me. It tastes kind of like fish and kind of like meat at the same time. Doesn't it, Ujurak?"

Ujurak nodded as if he wasn't really listening. His jaws worked as he chewed. "We're lucky Kallik found it," he mumbled around a mouthful. Lusa wondered if he was trying to remind Toklo of how much they needed the white bear's guidance out here.

She picked at the chunk of flesh she'd ripped off. She was excited about finally having food, but the rich, fishy smell was overpoweringly strong. When she bit into it, the dense, chewy fat nearly made her gag. It felt like eating heavy, fish-smelling slugs, all slimy and fatty in her mouth. She wished she could have fresh berries or grubs instead, but of course that was impossible out here. And she had to eat, or she would starve.

"Don't you like it?" Kallik fretted. "Just imagine it's a plump rabbit."

Lusa bit off another mouthful. "Mmm," she said, pretending to savor it. "You're right, it's just like rabbit. Um, only better!"

Satisfied, Kallik turned back to her portion. Lusa felt guilty for lying to her, but she didn't want Kallik to worry that she would go hungry out here. She forced herself to take a few more bites, chewing slowly to make it go down more easily.

"Hey!" A strange voice interrupted them, and Lusa whirled around to see a large female bear stalking toward them. "That's *mine*! I caught it!"

"Too bad," Toklo growled. "It's ours now."

"You can't leave newkill and just expect it to be there when you get back," Kallik said, planting herself between the seal and the unfamiliar bear.

"But—" the other bear started.

"Where is it, Mother?" a younger voice cried plaintively behind her. A small cub came scrambling over the top of the snowy hill and stumbled, tumbling down to land at her mother's paws. "I'm starving! I'm so hungry I could eat a—" She stopped, staring wide-eyed at the four bears around the seal.

"Hey!" she whispered loudly. "Why are those bears such funny colors? What's wrong with them?"

"It doesn't matter," said the she-bear. She stood up on her hind legs and clawed at the air. "They're going to back off and let us have our seal."

"No!" Toklo snarled, raising himself onto his hind legs as well.

Lusa exchanged glances with Ujurak and guessed that he felt as bad as she did. They were so hungry—but how could they steal from a tiny cub?

Suddenly a roar split the air and Lusa nearly jumped out of her skin. A full-grown male white bear charged across the snow toward them, baring his teeth.

Lusa's heart pounded with terror. How had he snuck up on them? He must have been moving very fast. He was *enormous*, and from the look on his face, he wasn't very pleased.

"I SMELL SEAL AND IT WILL BE MINE—" The white bear stopped midroar and skidded to a halt. He stared at the brown and black bears.

"What—how—" he stammered. He shook his head vigorously and pawed at his eyes. He swung his head toward Kallik and the other white bear. "Are those *brown* bears? And a black bear? Out here on the ice?"

"Yes," Kallik said, her voice trembling a little. She lifted her head and looked him straight in the eye. "Yes. They're my friends."

"Your *friends?*" he barked. "What are they doing out here? They'll never survive!"

Toklo gave Lusa an *I told you so* expression.

"They will!" Kallik said fiercely. "I'll make sure they do!"

"So will I!" Ujurak jumped in, looking angry.

The grown bear's gaze fell on the half-eaten seal. "By helping them to steal other bears' newkill?" he growled. "There's barely enough for the white bears to eat out here. And now you're bringing strange bears who don't belong to steal our prey?"

"We're not stealing! We have as much right to this newkill as anyone," Kallik snapped. "Certainly as much as you. You didn't catch it, either!"

Ujurak suddenly reared up on his hind legs. "And if you disagree, you can fight us for it, bear to bear!"

"Ujurak, no!" Lusa squeaked. She saw the mother bear nudging her cub backward out of the way. The cub's tiny paws were trembling with fear.

The male bear reared up on his hind legs as well, lashing out at Ujurak with one of his front paws. Ujurak dodged the blow and then threw himself at the bigger bear, bashing into his stomach with his shaggy head. His claws raked down the white bear's side, leaving thin trails of red blood. The bear roared angrily, flung out a huge paw, and thwacked Ujurak on the side of the head. He flew through the air and landed with a painful thud on the ice. He crumpled into a furry heap and lay still and unmoving. Lusa couldn't even see him breathing.

The male bear charged over and reared up, preparing to crush him with his massive paws.

"Ujurak!" Lusa screamed.

A blur of brown and white fur shot past her, and she shrank back as Kallik and Toklo both leaped at the giant white bear. Toklo's jaws fastened in the bear's neck and he sank his claws in to hold on, growling ferociously. Kallik reared up on her hind legs and battered his head with her paws.

Terrified, Lusa scrambled behind a lump of ice and covered her head with her paws. She couldn't watch. The bear was so big! And as they fought, she could feel the ice shaking beneath them. What if it cracked, and they all fell in? Who would save her if they all died?

Lusa heard a deep growl and the trembling stopped. She peeked out and saw that the giant white bear had finally shaken Toklo off. He backed away as Toklo and Kallik stepped toward him, brown and white fur side by side. As scared as she was, Lusa felt a burst of pride. They weren't afraid of anything!

"It's not worth it," the white bear spat, glaring at the cubs. "I'm not going to fight you over a scrap of seal skin. If you

want to share your food with bears who don't belong here,
that's your problem," he said to Kallik. He cast a scornful look
at Lusa, Toklo, and Ujurak. "Black and brown bears don't
belong on the ice. Everyone knows that. You only have to look
at their fur to know that. Muddy, sticky bears." He shuddered.
"You'll find that out soon enough!"

He turned and bounded across the snow, disappearing
quickly into the blinding whiteness.

Lusa galloped down to Ujurak's still body, reaching it a
moment before Toklo and Kallik did. "Ujurak!" she yelped,
pressing her nose into his fur. "Are you all right? Ujurak!"

To her relief, he drew a long, shuddering breath and struggled to sit up.

"What were you thinking?" Toklo exploded. "Picking a
fight with a full-grown white bear all by yourself? You could
at least have transformed into a white bear before you did it,
you squirrel-brained—"

"No!" Ujurak snapped. "I'm a brown bear! I'll fight like
one! And we need food, so why shouldn't I help defend it?
That's what brown bears do, isn't it?" He licked his shoulder
and winced a little.

Lusa couldn't believe Ujurak was behaving so oddly. He
never chose violence if he could avoid it.

"Why don't you let us do the fighting from now on?" Kallik
suggested.

Ujurak bridled, and Lusa jumped in quickly. "It's not that
we don't think you're strong, Ujurak! It's just that if anything
happened to you, we'd all be lost—we wouldn't know where

to go or what to do. The quest would be over. Can't you see that?"

A tense moment passed, and then Ujurak swiped at the snow with his front claws. "Fine," he muttered.

Suddenly Toklo gasped. "The seal!" he roared. "It's gone!"

"Gone!" Kallik shoved past him and stood next to the breathing hole. The ice was bloodstained where the carcass had been, but there was no sign of the seal itself. "How—where did it go?" She gave the dark water a puzzled look, as if perhaps the seal had come back to life and swum away.

"The mother bear," Lusa realized. "She must have snuck off with it while you were fighting."

"How *dare* she!" Toklo roared.

"Well, it was hers to begin with," Lusa pointed out.

"Only until we claimed it," Toklo retorted. "You should have been keeping an eye on it!"

"Oh, right!" Lusa flared. "Because I'm so sure *I* could have stopped her! With what, my useless tiny paws?" She scuffed a pawful of snow at him and turned her back, huffing angrily.

There was a long moment of silence, and then Kallik sidled up to Lusa. "It's not your fault," she said in a quiet voice. "You don't need to be scared of other white bears. We'll protect you."

"I know that," Lusa mumbled. "You were brilliant, Kallik. I'm fine."

But she was lying again. Seeing that white bear, and hearing what he said about her fur, made her feel even more uncomfortable than before. She hadn't even thought about how she stood out against the snow. White bears could probably see her coming for skylengths and skylengths. Or if their noses were like Kallik's, they could almost certainly *smell* her.

"Let's keep going," Ujurak said, stalking up the hill in the direction the mother bear had gone. Lusa could smell the trail of the seal carcass, but she was glad Toklo didn't suggest going after it. She couldn't bear the thought of eating now anyway.

Kallik bounded ahead to take the lead with Toklo close behind her. Lusa followed with a sigh. She tried to look on the bright side: They'd chased off a big white bear on their own. And maybe they wouldn't have to be out here too much longer. Maybe they'd figure out what they had to do, save the wild, and return to the land again.

Best of all, maybe soon night would fall, and then Lusa would be able to go back to sleep.

CHAPTER NINE

Kallik

A *cold night wind blew across* the ice, but inside another cave of snow, Kallik was warm and cozy. She watched Lusa's back slowly rise and fall as the little black bear slept. In their huddled sleeping pile, it was hard to tell which fur was Toklo's and which was Ujurak's. Kallik had a sharp burst of memory of Nisa and Taqqiq sleeping curled together in the same way. It was so powerful she could almost smell her mother's warm breath and feel her brother's solid bulk pressed against her side.

Her mother's spirit felt so close to her, out here on the ice. Nisa seemed to be watching her from every ice bubble, from the light drifts of snow dust in the wind, from the bright, sparkling ice spots in the sky.

Kallik shifted her weight. The sun wouldn't be up for a little while yet, but she couldn't fall asleep again. She was too happy to be on the ice and surrounded by snow. And she felt responsible for the others—in her dreams, she walked in Nisa's pawsteps, worrying about Toklo, Ujurak, and most of all Lusa as if they were her own cubs.

She just hoped that Ujurak was right to have faith in her, and that her instincts were taking them the right way.

Perhaps she could try catching a seal while the others slept. Carefully she eased her paws free and dug at the tunnel she'd filled in. A gust of cold air swept in and Toklo rolled over in his sleep, grumbling. Kallik nosed her way outside and shoved snow back into the hole to keep the others warm.

The night was very quiet, with moonlight casting a peaceful glow over the empty ice. Kallik's white fur ruffled in a breeze that carried gusts of snow into swirling whirlwinds around her head. She lifted her muzzle and inhaled deeply. Through the sharp, pure smells of ice and snow came the warm, furry scent of seal. She began to pace toward it, wondering if she looked as powerful and graceful as she remembered Nisa looking when she hunted. Snow crunched under her paws, and she let out a satisfied huff. It was good to have clean fur again, after moons of dirt clogging up her pads.

The scent led her across small hills of snow to a wide, flat part of the ice. Kallik spotted the breathing hole from a few bearlengths away, dark against the paler gray of the ice. Cautiously she crept up to it and settled down to wait, resting her nose on her front paws. Vivid memories flooded through her—of her mother waiting patiently, teaching Kallik and Taqqiq the importance of absolute stillness and silence. *Become one with the sea-ice*, she thought, hearing her mother's voice echo in her mind. *Absorb its stillness and the seals will not sense you.*

Without the other three watching her, Kallik felt focused

and sharp, all her senses alert. She felt as though she could wait like this forever, watching the hole and dreaming of her cubhood. Her breathing slowed as she sensed the comforting presence of spirits in the ice and stars all around her. She was so caught up in her memories that she nearly missed the hint of a splash right before a seal popped its sleek brown head out of the hole. It gave her such a startled look that she would have laughed, if she hadn't been lunging forward to sink her claws into its neck. She could already taste the rich fat sliding down her throat.

But to her surprise, her paws closed on empty air. With another splash, the seal disappeared below the water. She'd missed it! She'd failed again!

Kallik sat back on her haunches and stared at the dark water. She'd been so sure she was going to catch it. And this time she couldn't blame Toklo for distracting her.

Was it hopeless? Perhaps Nisa dying so soon meant that she would never be a real white bear. Maybe there was too much her mother hadn't had time to teach her. Miserable, Kallik trudged back to her friends. She wished her mother's voice would return and tell her what she was doing wrong.

The sun was a pale pink glow on the edge of the sky when she reached the snow cave and started digging into it with her paws. Toklo shot awake as she poked her head inside. He nearly clawed her nose off before he realized it was her and not an invading bear.

"Where have you been?" he snapped.

"Nowhere," she said. "Just walking around." She didn't

want to admit that she'd failed yet again to catch a seal. She could just imagine how Toklo would react to that.

As if he'd read her mind, Toklo said, "I am dying of hunger. Let's get these lazybones up and go catch a seal."

Kallik winced guiltily. Toklo poked Ujurak in the side and he rolled onto his paws, blinking as if he'd been dreaming about being another animal and was startled to find himself as a bear.

Lusa was much harder to wake up, but she finally dragged herself out of the den, and they gathered in the sun, shaking snow off their fur.

"A good day for traveling," Ujurak observed, sniffing the cold morning air.

"A good day for *eating*," Toklo grumbled. "If we could just *find* something to eat."

Kallik took a deep breath. "Ujurak, listen," she said. "I know you want me to lead us, but I don't know where we're supposed to go." Her confidence was badly shaken by her failed hunt. She had to ask him for help now; she couldn't keep pretending she knew what she was doing. "I mean, what are you looking for?" she went on. "A white bear would normally just wander the ice, eating seals and sleeping until burn-sky returned. I have no idea what you think we'll find out here, or how I'm supposed to lead you to it."

She lowered her head, feeling better for having confessed, but mostly feeling terrible for failing her friends so badly.

Ujurak gazed around at the ice, looking thoughtful. "It's all right," he said in his faraway voice. "Let me try to read the signs." He paced a few steps away from them, studying the sky and the snow.

Toklo snorted. "More signs. I don't need any stupid signs. I can tell you exactly where to go—to the nearest seal!"

Kallik nearly snapped at him, her anxiety and frustration boiling over, when she suddenly realized that Lusa was asleep in the snow beside them. Worried, Kallik nudged her in the side until the little black bear slowly opened her eyes.

"Lusa, what's wrong?" she barked. "Something is wrong, isn't it?"

Toklo came to stand next to Kallik, peering down at Lusa.

"I'm just, um . . . resting," Lusa said groggily, trying to sit up. "I'm all right. Nothing to, um . . . worry about." She gave up and lay her head back down on the snow with a sigh.

"Lusa, you don't have to pretend," Kallik said gently. "Please tell me what's wrong."

"I'm sorry," Lusa said in a small voice. "I'm just—I'm so tired." She put one paw over her nose. "And my tummy hurts," she said in an even smaller voice. "I'm sorry, Kallik; I think it's the bit of seal we ate last night. It feels all wrong in my belly. All I want is berries."

Kallik put her paw lightly on Lusa's belly. The black bear's words were slurred as if she was speaking through a mouthful of water, and her eyelids drooped while she talked. But she was getting as much sleep as the rest of them—more, sometimes— and they weren't traveling as far on the ice as they used to on the land. It didn't make sense for her to be so tired.

"It's all right," Kallik soothed. "Just rest for a moment, and we'll wake you up when we're ready to go."

"Thank you," Lusa said with a sigh, closing her eyes. Within a moment she was in a deep sleep again.

Kallik looked up and met Toklo's worried gaze. "Do you think she's sick?" she asked as Ujurak came padding back to join them. Ujurak looked from them to the sleeping bundle of black fur at their paws.

"Maybe," Toklo said, digging his claws into the snow, "but I don't see what we can do about it. Unless— Ujurak, is there anything you can do?"

Ujurak shook his head. "There aren't any herbs out here," he said. "Even if I knew what was wrong with her, I don't have anything that might make her better."

Kallik felt a stab of powerful guilt. Medicine was something Nisa had never taught her about, because she and Taqqiq had never been sick—at least, not that Kallik could remember. "If Lusa needs herbs, maybe we should go back to the land," she said, forcing out the words. She desperately wanted to stay on the ice, but her friend's life was much more important. "Maybe it was a mistake to come out here after all."

"No!" Ujurak said firmly. "This is where we are supposed to be, I *know* it. I don't know what will happen next, but if we have any chance of saving the wild, we have to be out here." He stood up, shaking the snow off his fur. "We just have to keep going. The signs tell me we should go that way." He pointed with his nose and then set off without waiting for them to argue with him.

Kallik exchanged glances with Toklo again. "That was

strange," she said. "Wasn't it?"

Toklo shifted his shoulders. "I don't know." He prodded Lusa's side, but she didn't move.

"I mean," Kallik hurried on in a low voice, "it's not like Ujurak to not care about his friends. Right? Isn't it weird that he's not more worried about Lusa? Maybe there's something wrong with him, too. It's like he doesn't even feel anything right now."

"I'm sure he is worried," Toklo said, wriggling uncomfortably. "But maybe he knows something we don't. As usual." He poked Lusa again. "Come on, time to go."

"Maybe you're right," Kallik said, although she wasn't entirely convinced. "Maybe when we save the wild, it'll save Lusa, too. And that's why it's so important. . . . That could be it, couldn't it?"

"Sure," Toklo said in a tone of voice that clearly said he wanted to end this conversation. Kallik decided to drop it for now. Perhaps he was right, and she was reading too much into Ujurak's behavior.

Together they managed to rouse Lusa, and the three of them hurried after Ujurak. The mounds of snow around them seemed to become flatter and smaller as they traveled on, until the ice appeared to stretch almost evenly from sky edge to sky edge. Twice Kallik thought she saw pawprints in the snow of other bears, although she wasn't sure how long ago they'd been left there. Once she scented another bear moving far off in the distance, but it was heading away from them.

She wondered why they hadn't seen more bears out here.

She knew white bears preferred to keep to themselves, so she guessed that full-grown bears used their long-distance sense of smell to avoid too many encounters with others. But she'd always imagined the Endless Ice as such a paradise that she'd expected to find happy, well-fed bears everywhere. It surprised her to find only a few pawprints here and there.

After walking for most of the morning, they came to a broken-up section where huge chunks of ice floated free in the pale blue-green water. It looked strange to Kallik; she could see that the broken section extended for a skylength in either direction, like a path stomped right through the ice. No bear could have left this shattered trail behind them. So what had made it?

She breathed in and gagged. The scent of the black, foul-smelling stuff was strong in the air, and the broken ice reeked of firebeasts.

"Maybe we should try to go around," she suggested.

Ujurak shook his head. "I read the signs, and I know this is right. We have to keep going that way," he said, indicating the ice beyond the broken channel. "We'll have to cross."

"Oh, no," Toklo said. "Not more swimming! Come on, the ice looks exactly the same in that direction as it does over there. Why can't we go this way instead?" He jerked his head at the empty ice to their right.

"We *must* cross," Ujurak said again, stubbornly.

Toklo growled low in his throat. "How do I know you're not just making this up?" he said. "There's nothing to tell you where we are out here. I don't think anyone has any idea where we're going."

"Do we have to have this fight again?" Ujurak flared. "Either stop arguing and trust me, or go your own way without us!"

Toklo stepped back as if blasted by the force of Ujurak's anger. "Well, I just might do that sometime," he muttered.

"It'll be easy to swim across," Kallik jumped in, trying to reassure Toklo. "I did this all the time with my mother and Taqqiq. Look how short the distance is between the ice floes. We'll be over on the other side in no time."

Lusa looked doubtfully at the water. She edged closer and dipped her front paw in, then pulled it out and shook it. "Oh, *brrrr!*" she squeaked.

"Swim fast, and it'll warm you up," Kallik encouraged her.

"All right, fine," Toklo said, marching down to the water. "At least there's plenty of room to come up for air here." He was about to launch himself in, when Kallik spotted something moving under the water. Was it a seal? She searched the water with her eyes. Her heart began to pound. There it was again—sleek, black and white, with fins . . .

"TOKLO!" she shouted. "Get back! Don't jump in! Get away from the water *now!*"

"Huh?" he said, stumbling at the edge. "But you said—"

"Orca!" she shrieked. "Get over here!"

Toklo spotted a black fin slicing through the water toward him and scrambled back to where his friends stood. For a heart-stopping moment Kallik saw her mother's death happening all over again. Terrified, the bears huddled close together, listening to the splashes and strange noises the killer whales were making only bearlengths away.

"We'll never make it across," Lusa whispered, trembling with fear.

"Yes, we will," Ujurak said. "We have to. There must be a way to get there without swimming." He lifted his head to look at the unbroken ice on the far side.

Kallik raised her head, too, studying the stretch of water where the orcas swam. Most of the floating ice chunks were large and close together. "We might be able to jump from one piece of ice to the next," she suggested. "Then we wouldn't have to go in the water at all."

"I like that plan," Toklo said. "No more going in the water. Ever again, please."

They walked along the edge of the ice for a short way until they found a chunk close enough to jump to from where they were. Broken pieces of ice floated in the water all the way across, like a path of smooth white stones.

Kallik went first, although the sight of the black shapes under the water made her paws shake and her fur stand on end. But she had to be brave for the others. She crouched at the very edge of the ice and leaped, closing her eyes. She landed hard on the nearest chunk, which bobbed and tilted underneath her.

Kallik dug in her claws and crouched down until the ice stopped rocking and she was able to balance for the next jump. As she sprang, the chunk shot backward, toward the edge, where the others waited with anxious eyes. This time she was ready for the lurch under her feet as she landed, and she stayed low, hardly breathing, until the chunk of ice steadied in the water. It was bigger than the previous piece, large enough to take all of them. Kallik decided to wait for the others.

"Okay!" she called. "Join me here!"

Lusa jumped next, slipping on the ice as she landed, but clearing the small stretch of water easily. She looked fierce and determined, gathering her haunches underneath her for the second leap. Kallik slid carefully back to make room for her, and to balance the chunk of ice so that it didn't tip her into the freezing water. Lusa arrived with a small grunt, and a flash of triumph in her eyes.

Toklo and Ujurak followed, their blond-brown fur flicking along their flanks as they plunged through the air. It was a squeeze to fit them all onto the second chunk of ice, but at least it was a lot more steady—though the water had started to lap over the side where Kallik stood. They'd made it safely across half of the channel.

Well, Kallik thought, *"safely" if you don't count the dark fins circling us.* She tried to shove that thought out of her head. Their ice floe had floated closer to the other side when Toklo landed, and another large chunk was near enough to jump to.

One at a time, they leaped again. This time Kallik went last so she could keep an eye on the orcas slicing through the water. By the time it was her turn, the pieces of ice had floated farther apart. She took as much of a running jump as she could, but as she pushed off, she felt the ice move below her paws, and she knew she wouldn't be able to cover the whole distance.

The water seemed to rise up to meet her, sucking her in,

and she landed with a cold splash that took her breath away. Frantically she swiped her claws at the shapes around her. One of them darted in and rammed her in the side, knocking the wind out of her. Another swept up from below and crashed into her shoulder, leaving it numb from the impact. Kallik could hear her friends screaming her name, but the water swamped into her eyes and she was thrashing about too much to swim straight.

Terror coursed through her as she realized she was going to die. She was going to be killed by orcas, just like her mother. She was leaving her friends behind the same way as she'd been left—with no one to take care of them, no one to guide them through this strange world. It would be her fault if they died, too.

Suddenly she spotted a pale shadow in the water—white where the orcas were dark. The water was churning fiercely, so she couldn't see it very clearly, but the orcas all moved away from it, whatever it was. Kallik squinted through the waves.

"Kallik, swim!" Lusa's voice carried across the water. "Hurry!"

"Over here!" Toklo yelled.

Kallik turned away from the pale shadow and swam through the space the orcas had left. She reached up and felt the claws of her friends digging into her fur, dragging her up onto the ice. With a final heave and a scramble from her back paws, Kallik shoved herself up and out into the air. She was alive!

Even better, this chunk of ice had floated close enough to

the other side that they could leap across safely to the unbroken ice. Kallik tumbled onto the snow and lay there, her head spinning. She was too exhausted and dazed to stand up and shake out her soaking wet fur.

"That was really weird!" Lusa puffed, licking Kallik's ear. "The orcas just seemed to back away all of a sudden."

"If they hadn't, I would have jumped into the water and fought them off," Toklo promised. "I was just about to."

"You can't ever do that!" Kallik barked. "You can't fight them, Toklo. Not even my mother could fight them. Promise me you won't ever try."

"But it seemed like *you* scared them off," Lusa said, her eyes shining.

Kallik glanced over at Ujurak, who had a knowing look in his eyes as he gazed at the water. He lifted his head into the breeze. "I knew you would make it," he said. "It's another sign. We're meant to be together, and we're meant to be going this way."

Toklo snorted. "Could you ask the signs to be a little less traumatizing next time?"

Kallik didn't know or care if it was a sign for their quest right at that moment. She knew what *she* thought the pale shadow had been.

Thank you, Mother, she thought, closing her eyes and resting her cheek against the cool ice. *Thank you for saving my life.*

CHAPTER TEN

Ujurak

As soon as Kallik was up to it, they started walking again. Ujurak tried to shake off the fear he'd felt when he'd seen the orcas attack Kallik. He knew that if she'd died, it would have been his fault for insisting they cross the broken ice.

And was he right about where they were going? He wasn't even sure. The signs out here were so strange. He was used to reading broken tree limbs and piles of rocks and the sound of streams burbling in the distance. He didn't know what to make of the shifting whorls of snow or the endless, blank emptiness of the ice, and that troubled him deeply.

He glanced around at Kallik's huge bulk, looming over Lusa's small, dark shape as they trudged side by side. It had been a relief to hand off the responsibility of leadership to her for a while. He'd hoped her knowledge of the ice would be enough to guide them wherever they were going, especially when he was so confused out here. But of course she knew even less than he did . . . well, she knew more about surviving on the ice, but she didn't know how to read the signs of their

journey, and of course she didn't know what they were looking for.

He barely knew what they were looking for. The strange
tugging under his fur pulled him forward relentlessly, so he
knew there was a reason to be here. He just hoped he'd recognize it when they found it—and that it would help them save
the wild, as his and Lusa's dreams had promised.

Ujurak turned his eyes back to the sky. The dancing lights
had been such a promising sign, but all they'd told him was
to go out onto the ice. They gave him no clues about what to
do once he got there. Even the Pathway Star confused him; at
night it was nearly directly overhead, so he couldn't tell if they
were still supposed to be following it, or if it had just been
leading them here, to the ice.

And during the day it was even harder. He squinted at the
thin gray clouds scattered across the dull blue sky. Earlier he'd
seen four distinct streaks of clouds, all angling in this direction, which he'd taken for a sign they should go this way. But
now the lines had blurred away, and his certainty had melted
along with them. There was nothing in all this emptiness at
the moment to convince him they were on the right path.

He clung to the thought of Kallik's mysterious escape from
the orcas. Surely that meant what he hoped—that they had
made the right choice and the spirits were with them. He just
had to have faith.

And most important, he had to act confident for the others. They couldn't know that he was even a little unsure; he
had to hide how much the ice confused him. If they knew

how lost he felt, they'd lose faith in him. Ujurak looked back at Toklo stomping along, muttering grumpily to himself as he sometimes did. Toklo's temper was already on edge; Ujurak was afraid the brown bear would seize any excuse to go back to the land.

If Toklo lost faith in Ujurak's guidance, there would be nothing to keep him here . . . nothing to keep all four of them together. And Ujurak was certain that was the most important thing. All four bears were essential for whatever was ahead.

He took a deep breath, trying to calm himself. The memory of how he'd nearly lost himself as a whale still terrified him. And now that he'd taken back the role of guide from Kallik, the weight of his friends' expectations lay heavily on his fur.

He had to be strong. He had to act sure, even when he wasn't. He had to watch even more carefully for signs and hold the group together, no matter what. He couldn't hope that Kallik would lead the way in his place anymore.

Everything depended on him.

CHAPTER ELEVEN

Toklo

Toklo stopped on a sloping bank of snow and looked back at the broken ice river in the distance. He could still see black fins slipping through the green water. He shuddered as he imagined vicious teeth closing over his paws.

Nearly losing Kallik had given him more of a fright than he wanted to admit. He couldn't rely on the white bear to take care of them. He needed to learn to catch seals properly and how to find shelter on the ice, in case he needed to take over for any reason.

He hurried to catch up to Kallik, scrambling past a sleepy-looking Lusa and a plodding Ujurak. Kallik's wet fur was drying quickly under the sun and with the brisk breeze; she didn't even seem very cold. Toklo had always thought his fur was the perfect thickness to keep him warm, but now he secretly craved whatever was keeping Kallik so comfortable out here.

"Hey, Kallik," he said, nudging her flank. "Maybe you could teach me your way of catching a seal, the way your mother taught you."

"Really?" she said. She swung her head around to look at him. "You really want to learn? It seems pretty boring at first. You have to be *very patient*."

"Well, I'm quite a patient bear," Toklo said. "I mean, that's what I'm known for."

Kallik snorted with laughter and Toklo checked behind him to see if Lusa had heard his joke. But she was a couple of bearlengths back, struggling through the snow with her head down.

"I want to learn," he said earnestly. "I promise to listen, I really will."

"And behave?" Kallik prompted. He nodded. "And not grumble?"

"I don't grumble!" Toklo barked. "I never grumble!"

"Oh, really?" said Kallik.

"All right, if we get through this lesson, and I do exactly as I'm told, then you say you're sorry for calling me a grumbler."

"Deal," Kallik huffed. She lifted her head and sniffed deeply. "We're in luck. I think there's a seal breathing hole only a skylength and a half that way." She nodded at the edge of the sky in a direction that looked exactly like every other to Toklo. He tried inhaling, but couldn't smell anything like seal.

"How do you *do* that?" he whined.

"Same way you can find your way back to places you've been before," Kallik said. "It's just something white bears are good at, smelling things that are far away."

Ujurak only nodded when Kallik suggested they veer

slightly out of their way to reach the breathing hole. The sun had crossed the highest point of the sky and was heading back down into night when they reached the place Kallik had smelled. Dark clouds were gathering in the blue above them, warning of more snow to come.

This breathing hole looked small to Toklo, and he wished he could make it bigger, but he remembered what a bad idea that had been last time. So he followed Kallik, walking exactly as she did, sliding his paws carefully over the ice and then lying down right next to the hole with his ears pricked, watching for seals.

He could sense Lusa and Ujurak behind them, curled up together in the snow, but he tried to focus all his concentration on the hole, just as Kallik was doing. They waited and waited and waited for even a flicker of movement . . . but nothing happened. Not even a whisker of a seal broke the surface of the dark water.

Finally Kallik sat up with a sigh. The sun had nearly reached the edge of the sky, and the heavy gray clouds were thick above them, casting shadows ahead of the night. "I'm sorry, Toklo," she grunted. "You've been very patient, but this is longer than I've ever waited before."

Toklo scraped his claws along the ice in frustration. That wasn't fair! How could he learn to hunt if they couldn't even be sure there'd be seals where he was hunting? He turned to look at the other two waiting bears.

"Hey, Ujurak!" he called. "I have an idea! Come here!"

Warily Ujurak stood up and padded over to the hole. Lusa

shifted slightly where he'd left her, but didn't wake up.

"Kallik says there might not be any seals here at all," Toklo explained. "So I was thinking, maybe you could turn into a seal and just check for us."

"I'm not a piece of prey, Toklo," Ujurak snapped. "I'm a bear!"

"All you have to do is dive down there, swim around a bit, see if you spot any, and then come back and tell us. It'll be so easy. All right?"

"No!" Ujurak cried. "How can you ask me to do something like that?"

"It's no big deal," Toklo insisted, surprised by Ujurak's reaction. "We just want to know if it's worth waiting here any longer. It's not like we're asking you to lure them back here or anything."

Ujurak's eyes stretched wide amid the snow-flecked brown fur. "You don't understand!" he spat. "When I'm a different animal, I feel everything that animal feels—their hunger, their worries, their fears. I wish I couldn't do it at all."

"Hey, I never said I understood," Toklo argued. "All I'm saying is, maybe your changing could be useful once in a while, instead of just a nuisance, like it usually is."

"It won't take you a moment to pop down and look," Kallik added.

"Besides, you did it before with the geese, remember?" Toklo prompted.

"Oh, right, and that turned out really well! I nearly died!" Ujurak huffed. "That's exactly what I mean! What if something happens, or I forget to change back?"

"That would be stupid," Toklo said. "Just remember you're not really a seal. How hard can that be?"

"I'm a brown bear!" Ujurak shouted. "Okay? That's all I am, and all I want to be! A brown bear!" He turned and stomped off, planting himself in the snow next to Lusa with his back to Toklo.

Toklo blinked and gave Kallik a quizzical look. "What's gotten under his fur?"

Kallik shrugged. "Maybe being a whale for so long frightened him. Anyway, we can't force him, and I don't think we should wait here much longer." She nodded at the sky. "A storm is coming. We should find shelter . . . and hopefully the hunting will be better farther from the shore."

Toklo's stomach spasmed painfully with hunger. He had no idea where the shore was from here. Could Kallik smell that, too? Was it close—and what did "close" mean to a white bear who could run several skylengths in a day?

They trudged back over to the others. Ujurak got up when he heard them approaching and stomped a few paces off into the snow, glaring over his shoulder at Toklo.

Lusa lifted her head sleepily. "What happened?" she asked with a yawn.

"Nothing," Toklo said. "Come on, up you get." He nudged her to her paws. "We're going to find shelter."

"Shelter where we can sleep?" Lusa said hopefully.

"That is the general idea," Toklo said, shaking his head at her.

As Kallik took the lead again, it began to snow harder. Fat snowflakes drifted down into their fur, catching on their noses and ears. They padded past low hillocks of snow and jagged claws of ice that looked as if they were trying to snag the clouds. Gradually the wind picked up, howling across the ice, so the bears had to huddle close together to make sure they weren't swept apart.

Kallik lifted her head and stopped abruptly. "I smell another white bear," she said. "She's very close—I didn't smell her before, because of the storm."

"Does she have prey?" Toklo asked. "Maybe we could chase her off, like we did the last one."

"I don't want to do that," Kallik said, looking uncomfortable. "We shouldn't need to steal food from other bears. We should be able to catch our own." She sighed and shook off some of the snow that was drifting across her back. "Shelter is more important right now, anyway. We need to find a place to build a den." She gave the sky a worried glance and started forward again.

"What about one of these?" Toklo suggested, batting at a large mound beside them. It looked to him like there were plenty of snowdrifts to shelter in, stretching to the edge of the gray, stormy sky. But to his surprise, when he prodded them he realized the snow was only a thin layer covering a solid block of ice. He scraped at the ice with his claws, but it was hard as rock. Frustrated, he tried digging harder, but then his paw slipped and the ice scratched his pad. He jumped back with an outraged yelp.

"OW!" He licked his paw. A few drops of blood dripped onto the snow.

"You seal-brain," Kallik said, whirling on him angrily. "Don't you know a white bear will be able to smell that from skylengths away?" She jabbed at the drops of blood with her claw. "They'll come sniffing around looking for us—and if prey is hard to come by, they might settle for one of us instead of a seal."

Toklo was about to snap back at her, when his eyes fell on Lusa. He remembered how larger brown bears had thought of him as prey when he was a small cub. White bears were even bigger than full-grown brown bears. And Lusa looked tiny and vulnerable out here on the ice. If anything happened to her, and it was his fault . . .

He swallowed his angry response and quickly covered over the blood spatters with fresh snow. The storm was getting worse, and the blood drops were soon hidden. He dug his paws into the snow until they went numb and the bleeding stopped. He would never risk bringing danger down upon his friends.

"These mounds aren't big enough anyway," Kallik said, shouting to be heard over the roaring wind. "We need a taller snowdrift, one we can really dig into, and it can't be frozen all the way through."

They started walking again, fighting through the blizzard. Kallik poked the hills of snow they passed to see if any would suit as a den. Toklo bowed his head to keep the snow out of his eyes, wishing he could keep it from swirling in his ears.

He thought it must be even tougher for Lusa, with her big, round ears. His large paws were having enough trouble in the deep snow; her little ones must be sinking up to her belly. He turned to check on the small black bear . . . and discovered that she had vanished.

"Kallik!" he roared. Up ahead, Kallik and Ujurak both stopped and turned around. They were only shadows in the snowstorm, although they couldn't be more than a bearlength or two ahead of him. How would they ever find Lusa in this?

"Lusa's missing!" Toklo barked. "She's not behind me anymore!" He turned and floundered back through the gathering snow. What if a white bear had snuck up behind them, grabbed Lusa, and run off with her? Or what if she had slipped into a crack in the ice and the storm had carried away her cries for help?

Horrible pictures crowded through his mind as he pressed forward, anxiously searching the snow along the path they'd come. He could follow their pawprints for a way, but the snow was already covering them with terrible speed. If they lost the path they'd taken, they might never find Lusa.

"Toklo, wait!" Kallik called, bounding up beside him. "I can smell her! Follow me!" She sped up, galloping into the driving snow, and he charged after her with Ujurak close on his heels.

Kallik skidded to a stop near a small pile of snow. Gently she poked the snow with her nose, then brushed some of it aside with her paw. Underneath the snow, curled up against a drift, was Lusa.

She was fast asleep.

A jolt of fear shot through Toklo's fur. He looked up at Kallik and Ujurak with wide eyes.

"What is it?" Kallik asked, trembling already at the look on his face.

Toklo swallowed. "I think I know what's wrong with Lusa."

CHAPTER TWELVE

Lusa

Lusa felt the slow beat of her heart matching its rhythm to the heartbeat of the earth. She was warm and comfortable for the first time in a long while. The sun was hidden away, but its warmth seeped through her paws and her fur, promising that it would return. She was surrounded by the scents of bears she knew and loved—the familiar smells of Ashia, King, Yogi, and Stella from the Bear Bowl floated around her, comforting her. She saw the faces of Toklo, Kallik, and Ujurak, all at peace with the world for once.

That was how she felt: at peace. Everyone was safe. She breathed in the whole world, feeling connected to it through every whisker. Leaftime would come again, and for now she could sleep, waiting peacefully for it to return.

Then something sharp jabbed at her belly, breaking into the dream like an unwelcome burst of sunlight inside a shadowed cave. Lusa tried to wriggle away, but someone was poking her from the other side as well. There was nowhere she could escape back into her sleep. Gradually her breathing sped up, and she sensed cold, hard ice below her.

"Lusa! Lusa! Lusa!" Her friends' voices were too loud, too insistent. Lusa covered her head with her paws, trying to block them out. She wanted to go back to the peaceful place. She wanted to sleep.

"No, Lusa, wake up! You have to wake up!" Toklo barked, nudging her again. She could smell the seal carcass on his breath, meaty and rich. A fierce wind struck her nose, filling it with the scents of ice and snow. She shivered as a blast of cold shot through her bones. Why would her friends do this to her? Why couldn't they just *let her sleep*?

"Go away, Toklo!" she growled. She shoved his paws away from her. "You're ruining it! I don't want to be awake! It's nice and warm when I'm sleeping, so go away and let me sleep!"

"Lusa, you can't," he said, and the fear in his voice woke her up more than any of his jabbing and prodding. Snow flew into her face as she rubbed her eyes and blinked up at him. The world was a blinding whirl of white and the howling wind struck her with its full force. She didn't want to wake up into this storm, but Toklo hung over her anxiously. "You mustn't let yourself sleep out here in the open, Lusa," he insisted. "This isn't the right time or place. You have to stay awake."

Memories of Ashia saying the same thing in her dream came back to Lusa. She tried pulling herself into a sitting position, although it tired her out just to do that. "Why?" she yelped. "What—what's the matter with me?" She looked at Kallik, pressed up against her other side, and saw Toklo's look of terror reflected there. Ujurak was pacing in a circle around them, pawing at the snow on his face and watching her worriedly. Around them the storm still raged, and it was hard to see much beyond the shadows of her friends gathered close to her.

"It's the longsleep," Toklo said quietly. "Brown bears do it when the cold weather comes and the season of earth-sleep sends all creatures into their dens to wait for fishleap to return. They burrow into the earth and sleep through the cold months, until they can come out with the warm weather and find enough food to live on again." He shook his head, burying his black nose in her fur. "I didn't know that black bears did it, too. But that must be what's happening to you—you're feeling the pull of the longsleep."

"I can't believe I forgot about it," Ujurak said guiltily. "I should have known this would happen to you."

Lusa shook her head, trying to give Ujurak and Kallik reassuring looks. "That can't be it," she said. "I never heard about any longsleep in the Bear Bowl. Wouldn't my mother have told me about it, if black bears did it?"

"Maybe they do it only in the wild," Toklo said, and Ujurak nodded. "But you can't fall asleep out here, Lusa. You might not wake up again until the ice melts, and then what would you do?"

I guess I'd wake up once I hit the water, Lusa thought, but she knew he was right. If she woke up in the sea, skylengths from shore with no idea which direction to swim in, she would surely die. Assuming she even survived the moons of cold-earth out here, where any white bear might find her and eat her or the storms might freeze her to death without her even noticing.

"All right," she said, shaking herself so the snow flew off in swirling white clouds. "I won't let myself sleep. At least now I know what's wrong with me, right?"

She sighed. It was a relief to know that this was normal for a wild black bear. But it was scary, too. How could she fight the longsleep that was curled up inside her, waiting to wash over her like soft water? If this was natural for bears, what could she do to stop it?

As if he'd read her mind, Toklo nosed her gently and said, "I can feel the pull of the longsleep, too. I find it helps if I eat well and keep moving."

Lusa's stomach ached at the thought of any more seal fat. "I'll try," she said. "But it's hard to keep moving when it's so cold."

"We *have* to keep moving," Ujurak insisted. "We're wasting time here. We have to go."

"We're not wasting time," Toklo said, giving him an icy look. "We're making sure Lusa is all right."

"I know, I know," Ujurak said. He started pacing back and forth again. "But it's just a storm. We can handle a storm, if we just keep going."

"I will," Lusa promised, rubbing her face with one paw. "I can do it, Ujurak."

Kallik lay down and crawled up beside her. "Climb onto my back," she suggested. "I'll carry you, at least until we find shelter. We can't risk losing you again in the storm."

"And we'll figure out the rest tomorrow, after we've slept," Ujurak said.

Lusa felt her heart leap happily at the idea of more sleeping.

Even knowing how dangerous it was, she still wanted to sleep more than anything else in the world. That seemed like an ominous sign to her.

She scrambled up onto Kallik's wide back and flopped over like a cub. It was easy to tell from here how much Kallik had grown. The white bear's broad shoulders and hips comfortably supported Lusa's weight as they trudged on into the whirling snowstorm.

"Don't worry, Toklo," Lusa said. Her friend was padding right beside Kallik's paws, watching Lusa anxiously. "I've been sleepy before and managed to stay awake. I can do this!"

"I hope so," said Toklo.

But despite her words, Lusa felt Kallik's rolling gait slowly lulling her back into sleep. Her fur was so warm . . . Even the snow battering at Lusa's back didn't feel cold enough to keep her awake. And it was so easy to just close her eyes and sleep. . . .

CHAPTER THIRTEEN

Kallik

Kallik had her head down to keep the driving snow out of her eyes, so it took her a few moments before she heard Toklo calling her name.

"Kallik, stop," he said again, nudging her side.

Lusa's weight across her back was warm and heavy, and it took all her concentration just to keep putting one paw in front of the other. Reluctantly she stopped and swung her head around to Toklo.

"She's fallen asleep again," Toklo said, nodding up at Lusa. On his other side, Ujurak pressed closer and gave the little black bear a worried look. Through the whirling snow Kallik could see large shapes, like bears watching them, but she knew they were just frozen hillocks of snow and ice like the ones they'd been passing all day.

"There must be somewhere we can shelter around here," Ujurak said.

Toklo stared around at the bleak, dark landscape. "Even if we do find shelter," he said, "what happens if Lusa goes to

113

sleep and we can't wake her up again?"

They were all silent for a moment. Kallik knew none of them had any idea what to do if that happened.

She slowly lowered herself to her belly while Toklo tried digging in the nearest snowdrift. But before too long his paws hit ice. "It's like rock," he hissed, scraping it with his claws.

Kallik blinked, feeling despair wash over her. She couldn't search for shelter and carry Lusa at the same time. But they couldn't just keep walking forever, could they?

"We'll make her walk between us," Ujurak suggested, nudging Lusa until she slid off Kallik's back. Lusa's eyes popped open as her paws hit the snow and she stumbled upright.

"I'm awake!" she squeaked.

"You are now," Kallik said. "And you'll stay that way if you keep walking. Just one paw in front of the next, all right?"

Lusa nodded, rubbing her muzzle wearily. They set off again with the snow flying directly into their faces. The howling, freezing wind carried their voices away as soon as they opened their mouths, so it was impossible to talk. Kallik wasn't even sure how to look for shelter anymore. It seemed like every snow pile concealed a block of ice underneath. But if they stopped too long to search for one without ice in the middle, they'd be buried in the snow, and then they might never wake up.

Kallik's pelt brushed against Lusa's, although it was agony to walk as slowly as the little black bear needed to. She lifted her head to watch Ujurak as he paced ahead of them. His brown fur was almost entirely white under the snow. He pressed forward steadily, his hindquarters nearly disappearing in the flurries of snow between them. What was he looking for on the ice? What was Kallik supposed to find out here?

"Nisa, please help us," she whispered, but the wind yanked the words out of her mouth and scattered them into the storm. Surrounded by flurries of white on all sides, Kallik couldn't see the ice spots in the sky or the bubbles and shadows under her paws. She was utterly alone, cut off from the spirits above and below her.

She'd thought she knew the ice, but really she knew so little about it. All that time she'd longed to live on the Endless Ice—all that traveling to get here—and now it seemed as if she wasn't suited for it at all. Maybe she could survive better on land. Certainly she could keep her friends safer there. In this white, white world she couldn't even tell which way was up anymore. How had her mother survived with two cubs? How did any bear survive out here?

Kallik didn't know how long they walked, but her paws ached and her nose was numb and they were surrounded by total darkness and whirling snow, when suddenly Lusa and Toklo stumbled at the same time and collapsed to their bellies. Lusa buried her face between Toklo's front paws and curled into him.

"I can't go any farther," she said. "I'm sorry, I've tried."

"I can't, either," Toklo agreed, his breathing heavy and labored. "We have to rest."

"No, we can't!" Ujurak cried, bounding back to them. His movements were slow and exhausted, but he shook his head insistently. "We can't give up. Our quest—"

"I don't care about your stupid quest!" Toklo snapped. "We're trapped out here in a blizzard because *you* thought it was a good idea to follow *her*." He jerked his chin at Kallik.

A pang of guilt shot through Kallik. "I'm doing my best!" she protested.

"This is what the signs said to do!" Ujurak reminded him.

"You haven't caught a seal," Toklo pointed out to Kallik, ignoring Ujurak. "You can't find us shelter. You can't survive out here any better than we can! We might as well be following a salmon!"

"Stop fighting," Lusa murmured, burrowing farther into Toklo's fur.

"You just can't stand letting someone else lead," Kallik growled, getting angry now. "I'd be doing fine out here if I weren't dragging your worthless carcass around behind me. And you'd be dead if it weren't for Ujurak."

"We're supposed to be working together!" Ujurak yelped. "Why can't you all see that? We *have* to keep going!"

"For what?" Toklo snarled, turning on him. Lusa whimpered in protest as he shifted away from her. "To where? You don't even know where you're taking us!"

"Maybe I don't," Ujurak admitted.

A chill shivered through Kallik's bones. If even Ujurak didn't know where they were going, what hope did they have?

"But I know we have to get there, and I know we have to do it together!" Ujurak added.

"Do your precious signs say anything about how to stay

alive?" Toklo growled. "Because we're not going to be much use if we're all dead!" He stopped, panting, and looked down at Lusa, asleep between his paws. "I just don't care anymore," he said. "You keep going if you want to. Lusa and I are staying here." He flopped down beside her and closed his eyes. Almost immediately the storm began to cover them both with snow.

Kallik wanted to keep arguing, to try to defend herself, but the truth was she didn't think she had it in her to walk much farther, either. More important, she was afraid that Toklo was right. She had no idea what she was doing out here. She couldn't take care of her friends, even though she'd promised to.

She looked up and met Ujurak's hurt, confused eyes. "I'm sorry, Ujurak," she said. "I don't know what else to do. I can't find us shelter, and we're all too tired to keep walking. Maybe coming out here was a mistake."

Trembling with exhaustion, she curled up against Lusa's side and huddled as close to her friends as she could. After a long moment, she felt Ujurak lie down beside her, resting his head on his paws with a defeated sigh. The wind howled against Kallik's back, battering her fur. Perhaps she could protect her friends . . . if they kept Lusa in the center, maybe their warmth would keep her safe . . . maybe the storm would end soon. . . .

Kallik was asleep before she could have another worried thought.

In her dream, Nisa and Taqqiq were curled around her in

a warm den, listening to the storm howling outside. Kallik rested in her mother's fur, letting her fears drift away. Someone else could take care of her now.

"I'm going to get some food," Nisa said, standing up and rolling Kallik aside. She shouldered her way to the entrance of the den and began digging at the snow.

"Wait, don't go," Kallik begged. "We're all right in here."

Nisa didn't answer. Her white haunches disappeared down the tunnel into the whirling snow outside. Kallik crawled over to Taqqiq and huddled next to him. At least she wasn't alone.

Then Taqqiq stood up and walked to the entrance as well.

"Taqqiq, don't leave me!" Kallik yelped.

He shook his head slowly, then crawled outside.

Kallik was terrified. Why had they left her alone? She turned in a circle in the center of the den. It felt as if furry bodies were pressing up against her, but she couldn't see anyone else in there with her. She was on her own, and the den was filling up with snow.

More flakes flew in through the entrance, fast and furious as if bears were outside shoveling it in at her with their paws. But it wasn't ordinary snow. Kallik tried to dig into it as it covered her paws, but it was black instead of white, sparkling with the light from countless chips of ice, like the night sky turned into snow and piling up all around her. . . .

The ice spots swirled under her paws, eddying and rippling across the roof of the den. Kallik looked up and then all around, and realized she was surrounded by blackness on all sides. The den had vanished, and she was floating in warm darkness, lit only by the sparkling ice spots.

"Kallik," said a gentle voice.

Kallik turned and saw a great bear padding toward her across the sky. The bear's pale fur glittered with stars and rippled as she moved, carrying with it the scent of the wind. Her eyes were kind as she leaned down to touch Kallik's nose.

"Silaluk," Kallik breathed in awe.

CHAPTER FOURTEEN

Ujurak

The first thing Ujurak noticed was that he couldn't hear the storm anymore. An eerie stillness had replaced the howling, whistling wind that had filled his ears for so long. The freezing-cold feel of the snow piled up against his back was gone as well; instead he felt a soft breeze ripple through his brown fur.

Next to him, Kallik murmured something he couldn't hear. Then he heard Lusa's voice more clearly. "Arcturus!" she whispered.

Ujurak opened his eyes. The endless white of the storm had vanished. Even the snow under their paws was gone; the four bears floated in darkness, curled together just as they had lain down. The other three were asleep, although their ears twitched and they made soft noises as if they were dreaming.

An enormous shadow shifted in the darkness as if it was stepping out of the sky. Stars sparkled along the edges of its fur as it moved toward him. Ujurak raised his head, blinking at the massive bear looming over him.

"Mother," he said.

Relief flooded through him. He felt safe for the first time in moons. The starlit bear lowered her head and nuzzled him. He wrapped his front paws around her neck and held on, feeling like a cub again, cherished and loved.

"My son," she murmured. Her breath was warm and carried the scent of green growing things. "You have come such a long way."

She drew him into her fur and he nestled closer, remembering how they used to sit like this when she was teaching him about life as a bear.

"I am very proud of you," she rumbled, licking his ear. "You have chosen your companions well." They both looked at the other bears, who slept on with peaceful expressions. Ujurak wondered how they could sleep through something like this.

"They're having their own spirit meetings," his mother said, answering his unspoken question. "To each of them, you look asleep, too."

"I forgot about you," Ujurak confessed, burying his nose in her fur. "I don't know how. But my memories—I couldn't remember anything for so long. I wasn't even sure if I was really a bear."

"Do you remember now?" she asked gently.

He nodded. He remembered sunlit days on a mountain, learning to hunt at her paws. He remembered her digging for herbs in a shaded grove, teaching him which plants could heal. He remembered her stories at night, when the stars spun dizzyingly above them.

He also remembered the first time he realized he could

shape-shift. They were in their den, dozing after a hunting lesson. A small brown mouse had crept out from the back of the cave, sneaking up to grab a berry that Ujurak had dropped.

Through his half-closed eyes, Ujurak watched it closely: its twitching whiskers, its black eyes flicking this way and that, its tiny claws scuttling over the stone floor, and its rapid, sudden movements as it darted from shadow to shadow.

As he watched, he felt a strange sensation, like itching all through his pelt. He opened his eyes wide in astonishment as his paws began to shrink. His tail grew longer and his ears opened up and out and his fur became less shaggy. The cave shot up around him as he grew smaller and smaller. He saw the mouse scurry away into its hole, squeaking in fright.

Finally the changes had stopped and Ujurak examined himself. His whiskers twitched and his eyes flicked nervously around the cave. The mouse poked its nose out of the hole again and peered at him suspiciously. After a moment, it trotted out and crouched beside the berry to continue eating it.

"Hello," Ujurak tried. It sounded like a high-pitched squeak to his big ears, but the mouse tilted its head at him as if it understood.

"I thought you were a bear," the mouse squeaked. "Peculiar. Guess my eyes are worse than I thought."

"Uh . . . yeah," Ujurak agreed.

"Berry?" the mouse offered, nudging the round, dark blue fruit toward him.

Ujurak scampered over and took a bite out of the berry. It was so much bigger when he was this size! Normally he'd swallow a whole pawful of blueberries in one gulp. But being this small meant he could savor the juice flowing over his tongue and really taste the berry. He licked his paws, wondering what else was different about life as a mouse instead of as a bear.

Then he had a troubling thought. What if he was stuck like this? Could he go back to being a bear? Would his mother know it was him?

"*EEEEEEEEEEEEEEEK!*" the mouse shrieked, fleeing back into its hole. "Run! A bear!"

Ujurak heard the mouse's sharp claws skittering away through the cracks in the stone. He turned around and looked up and up and up into his mother's wise brown face.

She blinked at him affectionately. "I thought this might happen. Remember you're a bear, Ujurak. A bear—come back to me."

The warmth in her voice was reassuring, and before Ujurak could worry any more, he felt himself growing and changing. His bear snout returned and his claws thickened and lengthened, and in a moment, he was a bear cub again. He scampered over and pounced on one of his mother's paws.

"Did you see me?" he barked. "I was a mouse! I went *squeak* and the mouse talked to me and he gave me a berry and I could hear all sorts of things and my whiskers were twitchy and I was a *mouse!*"

"I did see that," she said. "You're a very special bear cub, you know. Not all bear cubs can do that."

"Really?" He pawed at his ear. "I bet they wish they could.

Can I be anything? Can I be a bird, too?"

"You can be anything you like," said his mother. "But understand that you will sometimes feel very different from the bears around you. Try to remember that you're special and don't let it bother you."

Her words echoed in Ujurak's mind as he leaned against her paws in the starlit emptiness. He had felt so different . . . if only he could have remembered her words earlier.

"I wish we could have stayed together," he said sadly.

"Me too, little bear," she said. "But we cannot always choose the path we walk."

She wrapped her paws around Ujurak as he shuddered, remembering the flat-face hunters who had chased him and his mother with firesticks. He remembered the sharp cracking sound that made his mother fall to the ground; he remembered her telling him to run. He hadn't wanted to leave her, although he could hear barking dogs coming after them. But then, against his will, he'd felt his legs becoming wings, feathers sprouting through his fur, and a rush of air lifting him up to safety and freedom. He had tried to fly back to her, but although he circled for hours, he never found her.

"I missed you so much," he said. "I ate berries and insects and anything I could catch. Sometimes I changed into other animals, so I could eat what they ate, if it was easier to find. Was that wrong?"

"You stayed alive," his mother murmured. "That's the important thing."

"And then I heard a voice in my head," said Ujurak, lifting

his chin to look up into her starry black eyes. "I thought—I thought maybe it was you talking to me. It told me to leave the mountain and follow the star. I didn't want to—I didn't want to leave the place where I'd lived with you. I thought maybe I'd only be able to hear your voice in our place, and I didn't want to lose it and be alone again. But it told me I'd find other bears to join me, and they'd travel with me where I needed to go."

He ducked his head. "I still wouldn't go, though. It wasn't until the flat-face hunters came . . . and then a little brown bear saved my life, and I realized he would be the first to join me on my journey. That's how it began."

He turned to look at his friends. Toklo, who had saved his life more than once. Lusa, whose spirit shone like the brightest star in the sky. And Kallik, whose courage and loyalty never wavered as she led them on this final part of the quest. They had all done so much for him. . . .

"What is all this for?" Ujurak asked his mother. "Where are we going?"

She rested her chin on his head. "Be brave, little bear. Just remember what you have to do."

"But I can't remember that part," he said, clinging to her. "It feels like my head is full of snow when I try to think about it. I don't know where we're going, or why, or what to do when we get there."

"Keep heading toward the rising sun," she whispered. "I am waiting for you." She nuzzled his ear. "All will be well. I promise."

She nudged him back toward his friends, then lay down beside them, curving her massive body around all four of them to keep the blizzard at a distance. Warm, still air settled over the bear cubs.

"Sleep," she murmured in his ear, and Ujurak closed his eyes and slept.

Much later—it could have been moons later, for all he knew—he heard her whispering to him again. "I must leave you now, but we will meet again soon." He mumbled in protest, and she pressed her nose into his side. "Have courage, my precious son."

Ujurak opened his eyes and watched her walk away across a landscape that was now snowy and calm. Her paws strode across the snow, leaving no prints behind. Her starry outline blurred into the brightening sky, then vanished into thin air.

He pushed himself upright, blinking. The storm was over, but it had transformed the world. Instead of flat, featureless drifts of snow in all directions, the bears were surrounded by strange whorls of sparkling blue ice, looming over them in odd twisted shapes. Some of them looked like giant frozen waves, trapped in the moment before they crashed to shore.

"Wow," Ujurak said softly.

The other three bears stirred. Kallik woke up first, stretching her paws out in front of her and yawning. Toklo came awake abruptly, blinking and shaking his head. Lusa was the last to awaken, but she opened her eyes and sat up without needing extra prodding.

They gazed around at the weird ice formations for a

moment, breathing in the cold, still air.

Lusa let out a tiny, happy sigh. "It was Arcturus," she said. "The Bear Watcher. He was here, and he saved us! I saw him in my dream!"

Kallik shook her head. "No, that was Silaluk. *I* saw her. She's the great bear in the stars, the one who gets chased by the hunters all through burn-sky."

"I saw the bear, too," Toklo grunted. "The lonely one. The star we've been following."

"Actually," Ujurak said, "that was my mother."

The other bears whirled around to stare at him. Ujurak had never seen Toklo look more astonished in his life.

"Your mother has stars in her fur?" Lusa asked in a hushed voice. "But I thought that was Arcturus. . . ."

"I'm *sure* it was Silaluk," Kallik said. "She was a white bear, not a brown bear."

"She is all of these things, and more," said Ujurak. "But to me, she's just my mother."

"So what do you call her?" Toklo asked.

"I call her Mother," Ujurak said. Lusa woofed with amusement. "But I think she is sometimes called the Great Bear, and I'm the Little Bear."

"The Great Bear," Toklo echoed. "So your mother comes from the stars, and you can change into different animals. What *are* you, Ujurak?"

Ujurak inhaled deeply, letting the crisp scent of snow fill his lungs. "I don't know, exactly," he said. "But I know that Mother sent me on this journey, and we're nearly at the end of it." He turned his head to gaze at the distant edge of the sky. "She told me all will be well, and I believe her."

Toklo shuffled his paws and looked at Lusa sideways. Ujurak nudged Kallik's side. "We're supposed to walk toward the rising sun," he said. "I'm sure now. Everything is exactly as it should be."

He was anxious to move on . . . especially now that he knew that his mother was waiting for him at the end of their journey.

CHAPTER FIFTEEN

Kallik

Kallik's fur tingled as she turned her face toward the sunrise. The sun was barely above the edge of the sky, but its light already sparkled brightly off the snow, dazzling her eyes. The strange forest of ice spread all around the bears, some of the pillars as clear as still lakes so that Kallik could see the shadowy images of her friends reflected in them as they walked by.

She passed an ice whorl with two stumps jutting out on either side, like paws reaching toward her. It looked like a blue-white bear, jaws open in a roar of triumph. Kallik imagined Silaluk watching her from inside the ice, guiding their path.

A rich scent of fish and fur drifted past her nose and Kallik stopped suddenly, sniffing. "I smell seal!" she cried. She whirled around to face Ujurak. "I know I can catch it this time. Silaluk told me I belong here. She said that I have the spirit and courage of the greatest white bears. I want to try hunting again."

Ujurak gazed at the long rays of sunlight spilling through

the ice trees. "But it'll take so long. . . . I really think we should keep going."

"What?" Toklo growled. "Don't be a salmon-brain, Ujurak. We need food! Especially snooze-face over here." He poked Lusa's side with his claw and she jumped, blinking in surprise.

"What? I'm awake! What?"

"It won't take long," Kallik promised, feeling the power of the ice surging through her paws. "I can do this."

Reluctantly Ujurak nodded, and the bears turned to follow Kallik through the pillars of ice. The scent suddenly seemed very strong, and Kallik kept running ahead and running back to her friends because she couldn't control her excitement and energy. The rays of light from the rising sun lit up the ice like stars underpaw, and the wind tugged at her fur with the scent of more seals and more snow.

She spotted the dark hole in the ice in the shadow of a giant archway made of ice trees leaning against one another. The sun shone through the ice, sending shimmers of light across the rippling water.

"Wait here," she whispered to the others. "And *no fidgeting this time*. No helpful comments either," she added before Toklo could say something snide. He snapped his jaw shut and glowered.

Small puffs of snow rose up from Kallik's paws as she padded toward the hole. She crouched and slid on her belly the last few bearlengths, feeling the snow slide smoothly underneath her. This felt so much better than rolling in dirt all the time. At the edge of the hole, she braced herself and gazed intently at the water. The wind brushed softly through her fur, whispering with the voices of the spirits and the star-bear. Kallik couldn't believe that she'd really met Silaluk—and that Ujurak was her son! She remembered the star-bear's kind eyes and soft, wise voice. There was something about her calmness and strength that did remind Kallik of Ujurak. She was everything Kallik had imagined when Nisa told her the old stories.

Her breathing slowed as she focused on the hole. Her paws itched as if spirits were bubbling up underneath them, bursting to get out of the ice. But she kept perfectly still, watching and waiting . . . and then suddenly, much sooner than she'd expected, she was rewarded with a flash of movement in the water.

Instantly she leaped forward and sank her claws into the seal's blubbery flesh. The rubbery body thrashed under her paws, but her jaws snapped on its neck and the seal went limp. Thrilled, she dragged the carcass up onto the ice beside her, shaking it to make sure it was fully dead. Her mouth watered at the taste of the juicy flesh between her teeth.

She'd done it! She'd caught a seal, just like a real white bear!

Her friends scampered down the slope toward her.

"That was brilliant!" Lusa called.

Toklo's jaw dropped open when he saw the huge seal carcass, which made Kallik feel warm down to her toes.

"Nice work," he said, managing to sound admiring rather

than grudging. He settled down next to the seal and tore off a piece.

"I knew you could do it," Ujurak said, and in his voice Kallik could hear the echo of Silaluk's, encouraging her.

Kallik ripped off a chunk of flesh from the seal's belly and nudged it toward Lusa. "This is my favorite part of the seal," she said. "You'll love it. And hopefully it'll make you feel better so you won't be pulled by the longsleep today."

"Thanks, Kallik," Lusa said, but her short black nose wrinkled as Kallik pawed the newkill toward her. Kallik watched as Lusa bit off a small strip of meat and chewed slowly. The little bear's face looked pained, as if she were eating porcupine quills instead of delicious seal.

Disappointed, Kallik bumped her in the side. "You really don't like it?" she asked.

"I'm sorry," Lusa said, coughing and pawing at her nose. "I think it's amazing you caught that seal, I really do, but when I put it in my mouth I feel sick all over. I'm afraid if I eat it, my belly will only hurt more." She blinked mournfully.

Kallik looked up and realized that Toklo was standing next to them with a concerned expression. "You can't eat any of it?" he pressed.

Lusa shook her head and lay down. Kallik had to admit that her friend looked really ill now. She was thin and tired looking, and her fur was constantly damp from the snow, so she looked even skinnier.

"That does it," Toklo said abruptly.

Ujurak raised his head from the seal he was eating, his

attention caught by the determination in Toklo's voice. Kallik gave him an uneasy glance. That tone of voice usually meant that Toklo was about to do something he knew they wouldn't like.

"This isn't going to work," Toklo said. "I'm sorry about your quest, Ujurak. But Lusa and I must go back to the land . . . now."

CHAPTER SIXTEEN

Toklo

A twisted tower of white-blue ice stuck out of the snow to Toklo's left, nearly twice as tall as he was when he stood up on his back paws. It loomed over him like a warning, as if it was about to crash down on him and his friends.

Toklo didn't want to tell the others about his dream, which had apparently been very different from theirs. The gruff brown star-bear who'd come to him had been full of dire predictions. Toklo had woken with an oppressive, prickling feeling in his fur, and the strong sensation that it wasn't safe out here for any of them, least of all Lusa.

He'd tried to ignore it. No sensible brown bear made decisions based on stupid dreams. That was all they were. Just dreams.

But Lusa's illness wasn't a dream. If she couldn't eat out here on the ice, she would starve, even if they could keep her from falling into the longsleep. Every time Toklo looked at her, he remembered another little bear, sleepy and weak and unable to eat enough to fill his belly. Tobi. His brother had died; Toklo would not let the same thing happen to Lusa. Not if he could do something about it.

"Listen," he said, clearing his throat. "Uh. Maybe you did see your mother, Ujurak. And maybe you are supposed to go that way." He nodded at the glowing edge of the sky. "But I'm not."

"What do you mean?" Ujurak looked disbelieving.

"All I see is ice in every direction, for skylengths and sky-lengths," Toklo explained. "Only white bears belong out here. It's no place for black bears, especially ones who can't stay awake."

"I *am* awake," Lusa mumbled, without much conviction.

"I'm worried about her," Toklo went on. "Even if we can keep her awake, she's not eating the right food. She needs to get back to the land."

"But the star-bear!" Kallik protested. "You saw it, too, didn't you? It was a sign to all of us! We're being watched over by a very special bear who wants to keep us safe."

Toklo snorted. "Really? Do you feel safe? Does Lusa look safe to you?" He nodded at the black bear, who was trying to stand up and was swaying tiredly on her paws. "No, I'm not trusting my fate to the paws of a strange bear from the stars. We have to take care of ourselves. And for black and brown bears, that means going back to the land." He gave Ujurak a hard look. "You can do what you like, Ujurak, but my part in your journey is over. Kallik will be able to take care of you now. I'm taking Lusa back to the forest, where she belongs."

"No," Ujurak said, looking bewildered. "You can't leave us.

Didn't your dream tell you to stay? Lusa, what did Arcturus say to you?"

Lusa ducked her head and dug her claws into the snow. "He—I don't know, it was all so strange. I mean . . . he told me to follow my instincts. He said the wild would speak to me, and I should listen." She blinked rapidly. "But I don't know what that means! I thought it meant to go on with you, but now I'm not so sure. What if the wild is telling me to return to the land for the longsleep? What if not being able to eat the seal means that I'm not supposed to be out here at all?"

"You mustn't think like that," Ujurak said. "You are meant to be here, with us. I'm sure of it."

"I'm sorry," she said quietly. "I think the wild is telling me I need to live like a black bear. I want to go with Toklo."

Toklo felt a rush of confidence. It was nice to have someone admit he was right, for once. Kallik and Ujurak looked at Lusa with expressions of shock and dismay on their faces.

"But we have to stay together!" Ujurak cried. "We're so close now! My mother said we were meant to do this together, and she can't possibly be wrong."

"What happened to 'I'm just a brown bear'?" Toklo snarled. "Now it's all right to be some mysterious kind of star-bear, too? Well, *I'm* just a brown bear, thanks very much, and there's nothing special about me, and that's the way I like it. I don't want anything to do with star-bears or whatever strange spirit stuff you've got us mixed up in."

"Toklo, please," Ujurak said. "We can't do this without you two."

"Can't do *what?*" Toklo exploded. "You don't even know why we're out here! Where are we going? Are we just going to keep walking until the sky ends? This journey is flea-brained, and you know it."

"It is *not!*" Ujurak yelled. "My mother said—"

"If your mother is anything like mine," Toklo growled, "then we shouldn't be following her anywhere."

He felt a flash of guilt at the hurt look on Ujurak's face, but it wasn't enough to change his mind. The warnings from the star-bear echoed in his head, and he wasn't going to ignore them, even if it meant fighting with Ujurak. Especially if fighting with him was an easier way to split up the group than trying to explain what he'd heard.

"Fine," Ujurak said with a deep sigh. "Kallik and I will keep going to where the sun rises. Without you."

"Oh, Lusa, are you sure?" Kallik said, burying her nose in Lusa's soft black fur. "I'm worried about you, too . . . but I don't want to leave you!"

"I don't want to leave you, either," Lusa whimpered, "but I think I have to. I'm so sorry, Kallik. I really tried."

"I know you did." The white bear bowed her head, then looked over at Toklo. "The shore is that way," she said, pointing with her nose. "Just keep walking until you have to swim. It shouldn't take long to reach land from there."

"Good luck," Lusa said, turning to Ujurak. "I know you can save the wild, Ujurak. You don't need us."

The brown bear shook his head, but came over to nuzzle her affectionately. "Be well, Lusa. May the spirits guide your paws safely. I know my mother will be watching over you wherever you are." He glanced at Toklo. "You too, Toklo."

Toklo nodded, trying to calm himself down. He didn't want to leave on bad terms. "I hope we'll see you again one day," he grunted.

"Oh, I'm sure you will," Ujurak replied quietly.

As Ujurak and Kallik returned to the half-eaten seal, Toklo turned his back on the rising sun and led Lusa into the endless whiteness. He hoped Kallik was right that the shore was this way; it seemed no different from any other direction to him. Normally his sense of his place in the world was very clear. This disorientation felt muddling and unsettling. It just confirmed what he had thought all along: *Brown bears don't belong here.* He glanced at his companion, stumbling beside him up to her belly in snow. *Or black bears.*

Lusa often turned to look back at their friends as they disappeared into the edge of the sky, but Toklo kept his head resolutely facing forward. He knew that leaving them was the right thing to do, as surely as Ujurak seemed to know where he needed to go.

The sun rose higher in the wide blue sky, burning away the last few strands of clouds and sparkling across the ice and snow.

"I hope I can catch a seal," Toklo commented after a while. "Kallik's reactions must be very fast."

"So are yours," Lusa said comfortingly.

"In a river, perhaps," Toklo agreed. "But out here . . . well, white bears are made for hunting on the ice."

"That's true," Lusa sighed.

Toklo gave her a searching look. Her eyes were half-closed and her paws dragged along the snow. "Stay awake," he ordered, nudging her. "We'll be back on land soon, and then we'll dig you a den and you can sleep as much as you want."

"That sounds lovely," Lusa murmured. Another long pause passed, and he saw her eyelids drooping again.

"Lusa!"

"Well, talk to me, then," she said irritably. "Say something interesting enough to keep me awake."

Toklo snorted. "I'm not that interesting," he said.

Lusa bumped his side affectionately. "Tell me about what happened to you last night," she prompted. "You saw the star-bear, too, didn't you?"

"It was just a stupid dream," Toklo muttered.

"What did the star bear say to you?"

Toklo padded a few steps without saying anything. He didn't believe in star-bears. It was all nonsense. This was what happened when a bear spent too long on the ice. Suddenly he noticed that Lusa wasn't next to him anymore. He spun around and saw her slowly lowering her hindquarters to the snow.

"Lusa, what are you doing?"

"I'm going to take a nap," she announced. "Unless you tell me right now what that star-bear said to you."

Toklo galloped back to her and poked her with his nose until she stood up again, whuffling with annoyance. "You are one troublesome bear," he said to her.

"Oh, like you should talk!" she said. She tilted her head at him. "Well?"

"All right, all right, just keep walking," he grumbled. Pleased, she scampered alongside him, kicking up tiny puffs of snow. At least their little squabble seemed to have woken her up. He sighed. "Don't be afraid, okay?" he said. "It doesn't mean anything. But—the bear talked about danger ahead."

"Sure," Lusa said. It sounded as if she was trying to be brave. "Of course. There's always danger."

Toklo took a deep breath. "He told me that one of us was going to die."

Lusa froze in place. She gazed at him with wide, frightened eyes. "Oh, Toklo!" she breathed. "No wonder you were so scared!"

"I wasn't scared!" he protested. "Look at you. You're struggling out here. I've been thinking about this for some time, and it simply makes more sense for us to go back to the land. I don't need an imaginary star-bear to tell me that. So don't worry about it."

She bumped his side again. "I'm not worried." But there was a tremor in her voice that hadn't been there before. They walked for a while longer in silence.

Suddenly Lusa's ears perked up, and she squinted into the distance. "What's that?" she barked.

Toklo followed her gaze, then stood on his hind legs to try to get a better view. It looked like something large and dark and smooth-edged sticking out of the ice. He couldn't tell how large exactly. In all the white snow, it was impossible to tell even how far away it was.

"Should we check it out?" he suggested. "It might be food . . . or it might be dangerous."

Lusa's stomach growled. "Sounds like my belly thinks it's worth the risk," she joked nervously.

They padded toward the dark shape, watching it grow larger as they drew closer. It was much larger than a bear—larger than any animal either of them had seen before. It was even bigger than many of the flat-face dens that they'd seen. Toklo slowed down once they had a clear view of it. The sides of the creature were flat and smooth, swelling out between a pointed nose and a blunt tail. It loomed above them, casting a shadow that reached toward them like a pool of night spilled on the ice.

"It looks like a giant firebeast," Toklo whispered. "One of the floating ones."

"But it's stuck," Lusa said. She pointed with her nose at the heavy floes of ice that surrounded the firebeast's underbelly. "It can't go anywhere." They stared at it for a long moment. Nothing moved, on or around the firebeast.

"Maybe it's dead," Lusa said. "Like the one we saw near Smoke Mountain. Remember?"

Toklo nodded, picturing the decrepit firebeast they had found on a BlackPath. Like that one, this one had misshapen holes in its flanks and it slumped forlornly to one side. But it was much, much bigger than the other firebeast. It was more like a floating flat-face den, especially since it didn't seem to be alive. Toklo wondered if flat-faces had firebeasts to push around their floating dens, although he couldn't understand why they wouldn't just stay in one place if they had a nice, solid den to put there.

"Surely flat-faces don't live on the ice?" Lusa wondered, echoing his thoughts.

"Bah," Toklo grumbled. "Flat-faces get everywhere."

Lusa sniffed the air. "I don't smell any, though. Or hear anything like a flat-face. Do you?"

He shook his head. "It might be safe to explore it a little bit," he said reluctantly. He didn't particularly want to go near anything to do with flat-faces, but maybe there would be food hidden inside—food that Lusa could eat. If they found something that would be better for her than seal, he was willing to make an exception to his no-stealing-from-flat-faces rule.

Lusa clambered up the side of the ship easily, as if it were a tree in the forest, but it took Toklo a while longer, scrambling and grunting and digging his claws into the holes in the side. By the time he reached the top, Lusa had poked her nose into every crevice and was ready to scamper down into the dark interior.

"Careful!" Toklo called after her.

"Look at all this weird flat-face stuff!" Lusa barked.

Toklo hurried down a strange set of flat, shiny rocks, stacked so that it was easy to jump from one to the other. The light inside the floating den was dimmer than outside, but sunshine filtered through the holes in the side, drifting dustily over the empty spaces. It was almost as cold inside as it was outside. Icicles hung from the roof and white frost covered everything, shimmering in the muted light.

Lusa was in a large space at one end of a narrow tunnel, sitting up on an odd black flat-face thing with a tall back and a flat round seat under her paws. "Look!" she said when she saw him follow her in. She reached out with her paws and whacked the wall beside her. The thing she was sitting on spun around and around in place.

"Whee!" she cried. "How crazy is that! It spins!"

"I don't like it," Toklo grunted.

"Aw, you're just jealous," Lusa said, stopping herself against the wall. From her seat, she leaned her front paws on a flat brown surface with four skinny legs. Thin white leaves scattered as she nosed through them. They all had little black squiggles on them. Toklo stepped on one as it fluttered past him. Here the black squiggles were long lines, jagged along the edges, with a lot of white space in between. They looked almost like rivers or shorelines if you could look at them from far above—the way Ujurak described what he saw when he was a bird.

Lusa landed on the floor beside him with a thud, making him jump. "Let's see what's at the other end of the tunnel!" she suggested, scampering off to the far end of the den.

"How can you get this excited about flat-face things?" Toklo asked, following her. "Why is *this* what wakes you up?"

"Instead of your *fascinating* conversation?" Lusa teased. She poked her nose into the big space at the end. More flat surfaces and strange flat-face things. Lusa went over to something that looked like a wall to Toklo, but when she stood up and pawed at something sticking out of it, it popped open, revealing another space behind it.

"Ooooooooooh," Lusa breathed. Toklo crowded up behind her and saw that the small space was full of dried meat and fish, hanging from metal hooks on the ceiling. It was all frozen solid, covered in the same thin white frost as everything else.

Toklo stood up and clawed a large piece of fish down to the floor. It landed with a solid thunk, like a piece of ice crashing to the ground. "Can you eat this?" he asked Lusa.

"If we thaw it a bit first," Lusa said, breathing on the fish. They both rubbed it with their paws and breathed on it until it was soft enough for them to tear off pieces and eat it. Still hungry, Toklo brought down a few more chunks of meat and chewed through those as well.

"What do you think is in here?" Lusa asked, pawing at a little round container. It was small and Toklo could pick it up in one paw.

"Why do you think there's anything inside it?" he asked, sniffing it. It seemed like a solid block of flat-face metal to him.

"I've seen things like this before, in the flat-face rubbish," Lusa said. "But they were open, and there were usually delicious juices left inside."

Toklo was skeptical, but he picked up the object in his mouth and carried it to the wall. Hefting it in one giant paw, he smashed it against the wall as hard as he could.

To his surprise, it cracked open, and juice splattered across his nose.

"Fruit!" Lusa shouted joyfully. She dove on the tin, licking up the slivers of pale orange flesh that spilled out. "It's peaches!" she said, giving Toklo a delighted look. "I had these in the Bear Bowl sometimes. They're yummy!"

Toklo licked the juice off his nose and nibbled a bit of peach off the floor. It was sweet and juicy, but he still preferred meat. "I think I saw more of these somewhere—I'll go look," he offered. He walked around the edge of the room until he spotted a ledge high up on the wall. Several more small silver objects were stacked along it. Grunting with the effort, he scrambled up until he could reach the ledge and knock them all down.

One after another, he smashed them into the wall, and Lusa gratefully gobbled up all the fruit.

"It's like a black bear feast," she said, licking her paws clean. "I feel so much better, Toklo."

He stood up to peer out one of the holes in the wall. The shadow of the floating den had stretched even farther across the ice. It still shocked him to realize that the days were so short. "We might as well stay here for the night," he said. "It's sheltered, so we'll be out of the wind." Plus it would save tearing his pads trying to hollow out a chunk of snow. "And we can eat again before we keep going in the morning," he added.

"All right," Lusa said, padding out into the tunnel again. "I think I saw some soft stuff down this way."

"Soft stuff?" Toklo hurried after her. "We don't need—"

He skidded to a stop as Lusa charged into one of the small rooms off to the side of the tunnel. She leaped onto something long, fluffy, and white, and started digging with her claws until whatever it was was bunched up around her like a nest. Then she flopped down with a contented sigh.

"You're a crazy little bear," Toklo said, hopping up beside her. The fluffy stuff was weirdly soft under his paws, like sleeping on goose feathers or piles and piles of moss. He sniffed it cautiously, but any flat-face smell had faded long ago. *That's reassuring,* he thought. The last thing he wanted was for the flat-faces who'd lived here to come back and find him and Lusa sleeping in their nest and eating their food.

"Yup," Lusa said sleepily. She snuggled closer to him as he lay down. He rested his chin on her back and gazed out at the darkening sky.

"I hope Ujurak and Kallik are all right," Lusa murmured.

"Me too," Toklo agreed. He missed the weight of their friends pressed against him while they slept.

"It's colder without them," said Lusa sadly.

"I know," he said.

After a moment, Lusa's breathing slowed, and Toklo realized she was asleep. He saw a few stars appearing in the sky. This strange floating den, offering fruit and shelter in a place that had seemed so unwelcoming from the moment they set paw on the ice, had been a lucky find. But how much farther did they have to go before they reached land? Would he be able to take care of Lusa all that way? Would she be able to stay out of the longsleep until they were safe?

He shoved the words of the star-bear out of his mind.

No one was going to die. Not if he had anything to say about it.

CHAPTER SEVENTEEN

Lusa

A strange creaking sound woke Lusa from dreams of fruit and berries. She blinked at the pale morning sunlight. Toklo was standing at the window with his paws up against the glass, peering out at the ice.

CRRRRRREEEEEEEEAAAAKKKKKK.

"What was that noise?" Lusa yelped, sitting up and rubbing her eyes.

"I don't know," Toklo said, looking worried, "but I think we should get out of here as soon as we can."

"Can we eat something first?" Lusa pleaded. She jumped down to the floor and stretched. Her paws felt lighter and the pain in her stomach was gone. She felt well rested for the first time in days. She wished they could stay here longer.

"All right," Toklo said as she trotted to the door. "But carefully—and fast!"

Lusa scampered down the tunnel to the big room with all the food. She pawed open a few doors and dragged out some dried meat and fish for them to eat, while Toklo broke open more of the delicious fruit containers for her.

Lusa had her nose buried in a dripping pile of sweet pears, when there was another loud creak, and she distinctly felt the floor shift under her paws. She looked up in alarm and saw that Toklo had his paws braced wide apart. As they stared at each other, the floor shifted a bit more, and one of the unopened tins rolled slowly past them and clunked into the opposite wall.

"The den is moving," Toklo growled. "Let's go!"

Lusa lapped up the last bits of juice and scrambled after him to the door. They hurried down the tunnel, but just before they reached the way out, an enormous CRACK! split the air and the whole den tilted backward, knocking the bears off their paws.

"The ice is breaking," Toklo cried in a panic.

Visions of drowning in freezing black water filled Lusa's head as she galloped after Toklo, slipping and skidding on the sloping floor. They hooked their claws into the wooden branches that grew beside the steps and started to haul themselves upward. Lusa heard another crack and looked down to see a sharp opening like a claw scratch running across the floor below them. To her horror, water was beginning to swell up through the crack. She shoved Toklo as hard as she could with her nose and he climbed faster.

They burst out into the open, tumbling and sliding across the slippery top of the floating den. The sky was dim, with low clouds blocking most of the sunlight, and a strange, reddish haze hung in the air. The ice stretched around the den in a dull, forbidding way.

Toklo ran to the edge of the den and peered over the side. Lusa bundled up behind him and saw the dark water rapidly climbing toward them, as if it was sucking them in. The nearest ice was a bearlength away, and two bearlengths down. They would have to jump.

"I can make it!" she panted as Toklo gave her an anxious look.

"Then you go first," he said. Lusa didn't argue. She clambered over the side and inched her way down as far as she could. The water churned and bubbled only a few pawlengths from her fur. She took a deep breath and launched herself toward the ice.

"Ooof!" she grunted as she landed hard on the cold, slippery surface. For a moment she felt as if she was sliding back into the water, but she dug her claws in and hauled herself away from the edge. Quickly she scrambled out of the way and Toklo leaped down beside her.

They both turned to look back at the sinking firebeast. It was so huge, yet it was being swallowed up by the water as if it were nothing more than a berry. Loud popping sounds echoed from it, so loud that Lusa didn't hear the cracking of the ice as well.

"Uh-oh," Toklo said, shoving her back. She looked down and saw a large crack appearing in the ice at their paws. Toklo shoved her again, and they began to run as fast as they could onto the open ice, with the splintering, widening gaps chasing after them.

They ran and ran. Lusa hoped they were still heading

toward the shore; she was all turned around, but maybe Toklo had been paying attention. Her heart thudded as she thought about the ice splitting right underneath her and dumping her into the freezing water, where she might drown, or get trapped under the ice, or be eaten by orcas. The memory of their gleaming teeth as they snapped at Kallik made her run faster.

Finally Toklo skidded to a stop, panting, and Lusa crashed into him and landed on her backside. He turned to look back as she caught her breath.

"I think we're safe," he said. "The ice is more solid here. And I don't see the cracks anymore."

"Oh, good," Lusa puffed. She didn't know if she could have run any farther. She peered at the edge of the sky where they'd left the floating den. The large black shape had vanished, swallowed up by the water as if it had never been there.

"Did we do that?" she asked Toklo.

"I don't know," Toklo answered.

Lusa looked down at the bubble-filled surface under her paws. She shuddered. "Why did it happen, then?"

"Who knows," said Toklo. "Perhaps it was our extra weight pushing the den down. Kallik says the ice is thinner than it used to be."

"That's so sad," Lusa said, shivering. "Imagine if your home could just melt away. Poor Kallik. What if it melts and never comes back?"

She thought of her dream, of the vision telling her to save the wild. And what was she doing? Running off to the safety of the land and deserting her friends. She hung her head. It was too late to catch up to Ujurak and Kallik now.

She just had to hope that she was right, and that they didn't really need her after all.

CHAPTER EIGHTEEN

Kallik

Kallik's fur felt heavy across her shoulders when she woke up. She opened her eyes. Something was different—and not in a good way. She blinked, trying to chase away the blurriness of sleep. Nothing changed, and she realized that they were surrounded by a thin, reddish-brown haze drifting in the air around them.

Beside her, Ujurak shifted and woke up. He scrambled to his paws and wrinkled his nose. "What's that smell?"

"I'm not sure," Kallik said, sniffing and then coughing. "I've never smelled it out on the ice before." She pawed at her nose, thinking. "It smells like no-claw smoke, the kind that comes out of the firebeasts and some of the flat-faces' really big dens."

Ujurak clawed at the haze, looking puzzled. "But how could there be flat-face smoke all the way out here?"

Kallik shook her head. "I don't know."

"Maybe the sun will burn it off," Ujurak said. Kallik rose to her paws and followed him, paws crunching on the snow. It felt strange to be alone with Ujurak, without Lusa's happy chatter or Toklo's grumpy comments. Ujurak barely spoke. He kept staring off in the direction where the sun rose, as if he was straining his eyes to look for some sign of his mother out there.

There was nothing to see but ice in every direction. Toklo and Lusa had vanished over the edge of the sky the day before. Kallik missed them terribly, but if she really thought about it, she had to admit she thought Toklo was doing the right thing. Keeping Lusa alive was more important than forcing her to carry on with a journey that was making her sick. Kallik thought of Toklo's brother, who had died when he was still a tiny cub. Was that why he was so protective toward Lusa? At least Kallik hadn't had to watch her littermate die. She wanted to believe that Taqqiq had found his friends again, and had made it safely back to the Frozen Sea.

Instead of burning away in the sunlight, the reddish fog grew thicker as they stumbled forward. The bitter scent clogged up Kallik's nostrils until she couldn't smell anything else. It made her dizzy and frustrated, like having all her senses taken away. She couldn't tell where anything was anymore—the nearest seal hole, the closest open water—anything. She stopped and reached out with her paw to make sure Ujurak was still beside her.

"Do we really have to go this way?" she growled. "It smells like it only gets worse from here."

"We have to," Ujurak replied. "This is the way Mother said to go. What is this haze?"

"I have no idea," she admitted. "It's not a normal ice thing.

Um . . . maybe—" She hesitated, worried about how Ujurak might react to her suggestion. "Maybe you could turn into a bird and fly over the fog? Then you could see what's going on or how far it reaches. . . ." She trailed off.

Ujurak was shaking his head. "No," he said. "I know for sure now. My mother is a brown bear, and so am I. So that's how I'm going to stay. Mother will look after us."

Kallik sighed. "Don't you think maybe there's a reason you can turn into different animals? It would be really helpful. Just this once?"

"No," Ujurak said stubbornly.

Kallik rubbed her eyes and looked down at the snow underpaw. Here it wasn't as white and clean as it should be—instead it was stained with the reddish brown of the fog. "This can't be natural," she said. "What if the spirits are angry at us for leaving Lusa and Toklo?"

"We didn't leave them," Ujurak pointed out. "They left us. We're going the right way."

He pushed ahead, stamping his paws through the oddly colored snow. Kallik glanced up at the thick clouds of fog that seemed to be pressing down on them. If *she* could turn into a bird and get out of this, she would in a heartbeat. Why did Ujurak have to be so stubborn about not using his powers? She wondered what had happened under the ice, when he had turned into a beluga whale. Whatever it was, it had set him against changing shape ever again. Was it too much to expect him to share the suffering of every living thing? She felt a stab of sympathy for him. Maybe she wouldn't want to change into a bird after all. Being a white bear was good enough for her.

They trudged on for what felt like moons. Kallik couldn't tell if night was falling; she hadn't glimpsed the sun all day. Not only that, but she wasn't even sure they were still heading in the right direction. She had a terrible feeling that they were going around in circles. It reminded her of the stinging smoke she and Toklo had been lost in on Smoke Mountain.

"Ujurak!" she called. The small brown bear stopped and turned to her. "I think we should wait for the fog to go away," she suggested. "I'm pretty sure we've passed that big chunk of ice over there at least three times."

Ujurak squinted at the icy column she was pointing at. "That's because all ice chunks look the same," he said.

"Actually," Kallik said, annoyed, "they don't at all. That one has three stubby branches sticking out of it like a tree, plus a knobby bit at the bottom that looks like a root, and a hole at the top where the wind goes 'whheeet wheeeet' as it whistles through. I bet you couldn't find another piece of ice that looked exactly like that anywhere on the Endless Ice."

Now Ujurak looked impressed. "All right, you win," he said agreeably. "We can wait. I'm sure the fog will go away soon."

Kallik wished she could be so sure. She led him to a snow-drift near the tree-shaped ice. The snow was piled up higher than her head, so it gave them some shelter to curl into, although Kallik didn't like letting the reddish snow touch her fur. She turned in a circle, digging some of the snow aside to see if there was cleaner snow underneath.

Suddenly the snowdrift reared up and exploded toward

her. Kallik and Ujurak jumped back with a startled yell.

It was another white bear! The dense fog had hidden her scent, and she'd been lying half-buried in the snow, so they hadn't seen her, either. Her fur was streaked with the reddish-brown color, like bloodstains. Kallik looked down at her own paws and realized she, too, had red smears across her white fur.

"This is my den!" the strange bear growled. "You can't have it! My cubs need it!"

Kallik backed away a step. "We're not here to take your den," she whimpered. "I promise. We were just taking shelter from the fog for a while."

The she-bear collapsed against the snowbank, her whole body limp with exhaustion. Kallik realized that the she-bear could barely stand, even though she looked well fed, with a plump belly.

"Well, it's not quite a den yet," the strange bear admitted. "I'm resting right now, but I'll make it a den soon. Then I'll have my cubs in there and watch them grow until they're big enough to come out on the ice."

Kallik felt a twinge of sorrow as she remembered her own BirthDen. Her mother had built it before having her and Taqqiq, just as this bear was going to do. It had been warm in there, and cozy, and very, very safe. If Nisa had been too tired to dig her own den, she hoped a passing bear would have helped her.

"What's your name?" Kallik asked. "I'm Kallik, and this is Ujurak."

"I'm Iniq," said the bear. She squinted at Ujurak as if she was puzzled by his brown fur, but she didn't seem to have enough energy to ask about it. Kallik realized that Iniq's belly wasn't plump, but swollen with unborn cubs. She wondered if they were heavy to carry around.

Iniq pawed at the snow. "I want to start building the den, but I'm so tired. I just need to rest a bit longer."

"Let us help you," Kallik offered. "We're stuck here until the fog lifts anyway."

"It shouldn't be long," Iniq said. "I've seen this fog before— we call it dirty mist. It blows in with the wind from the east and usually disappears after a while." She looked down at the snow again.

"I'm a very good digger," Kallik told her. "I'll make a good den for you and your cubs."

"Really?" Iniq said, her eyes shining with gratitude. "You wouldn't mind?"

"We'd be happy to," Kallik said. "Right, Ujurak?" He nodded. Kallik dug a small hollow in the snow where Iniq could curl up, and then set her paws to the snowdrift. It was perfect for a den—tall, thick, easy to dig through—apart from the troubling reddish stains on the snow. Kallik dug with her big paws and packed the walls as tightly as she could. Ujurak tried to help, but he kept knocking over her careful piles, so she sent him to sit beside Iniq and keep her company.

The fog still hung around them. There was no change in the low level of light beyond the fog. Kallik tried sniffing to see if the no-claw smell was any lighter, but the thick scent of the haze hid everything.

She was packing the last bits of snow around the wall, when Iniq crept up the tunnel behind her. Kallik didn't notice until Iniq breathed out a happy sigh.

"I can't believe you did this for me," said the she-bear.

"Helping other bears feels good," Kallik said, glancing at Ujurak as he wriggled into the den behind them.

Iniq looked at Ujurak, too. "Are you—no, you can't be. I heard there were four."

"Four what?" Ujurak asked, his ears perking up.

"Well." Iniq looked embarrassed. "There's a rumor on the ice this season. . . . Other bears have been saying that there are four bears out here, traveling together. But only one of them is white—the others are brown and black! So I just wondered . . . because you're a brown bear . . . but maybe it's just a story."

"No, it's true," Kallik breathed. Other bears knew about them! "There was another brown bear and a black bear with us. But they've gone back to the land—it was too dangerous for them out here."

Ujurak's head drooped and he turned to the wall as if he didn't want Kallik to see the sadness in his eyes.

"I'm only alive because another bear helped me," Iniq admitted. "My mother died when I was very young. I thought I was going to die, too . . . but then I met a bear who let me eat the scraps of his prey. He didn't like to talk much. But at least he didn't eat me. And by watching him, I learned to hunt, too."

"I'm sorry about your mother," Kallik said. "I still miss

mine. She used to tell us all the stories about Silaluk while we were curled up in a den just like this one."

"Silaluk?" Iniq echoed.

"The Great Bear in the stars," Kallik explained. She felt a shiver in her fur as she remembered that that was Ujurak's mother.

"I don't know those stories," Iniq said, lying down on the snow. Her eyes clouded with sorrow. "I have nothing to tell my cubs."

Kallik took a deep breath. She could smell that the fog was still heavy outside. "I could tell you about Silaluk, if you want," she offered.

"Really?" said Iniq, lifting her nose a little way off the floor. "But you've already been so kind. . . ."

"I'd like to," Kallik insisted, settling down next to Iniq so their fur brushed together. "I haven't told these stories in a long time. Let me think about how it begins . . . oh, I remember.

"A long, long time ago, long before bears walked the earth, an enormous river of ice shattered into pieces, scattering tiny bits of ice across the darkness of the sky. Each of those spots of ice became the final home for the spirit of a white bear. If you are good, and brave, and strong, one day your spirit may join them." She woofed with amusement. "That's how my mother always started, anyway, with me and my brother."

She thought for a moment, then went on. "When you look carefully at the sky, you can see a pattern of stars in the shape of the Great Bear, Silaluk." Kallik glanced at Ujurak, who was listening quietly with his paws tucked under him. His eyes shone when she talked about his mother. "She is running around and around the Pathway Star."

Kallik paused, but no one said anything. This was normally where Kallik herself, when she was a cub, would have jumped in to start asking questions, but of course Iniq and Ujurak didn't know which questions to ask.

"Silaluk is being chased by three hunters," Kallik went on. She shivered as she thought of the no-claw hunters who had chased her and her friends over Smoke Mountain. "The hunters are Robin, Chickadee, and Moose Bird, and they chase her for many moons, all through the warm days, until the end of burn-sky. Then, as the warmth begins to leave the earth, they finally catch up to her and strike the fatal blow with their spears. The blood of the Great Bear falls to the ground, and everywhere it falls the leaves on the trees turn red and yellow."

Kallik heard a small intake of breath from Ujurak. Even though it was a story, she could imagine that he didn't like hearing about his mother's death. She hurried on to the rest of it.

"Silaluk dies, but she doesn't stay dead. All through the long, cold months of snow-sky, Silaluk's skeleton lies buried under the ice. But then burn-sky returns, and the Great Bear is reborn as the ice melts and the bear spirits are freed into the sky. And then the three hunters gather, and the hunt begins all over again."

"Wow," Iniq said in a hushed voice. "Your mother must have been very wise. You were lucky to have her."

"Your cubs will be lucky with you, too," Kallik said. "You can tell them that story and show them Silaluk in the sky. Just look for the stars in the shape of a bear, circling the brightest star in the sky—that's the Pathway Star." Kallik turned to Ujurak, wondering what he was thinking. She half expected him to tell her that the stories were all wrong, that nothing like that had ever happened to his mother. She wasn't sure she wanted to know if the stories weren't true.

But Ujurak just murmured, "The Great Bear is all things to all bears. That's what makes her so important." He leaned against the snowy wall and closed his eyes. Kallik wondered if he was missing his mother as much as she missed Nisa.

She looked down at her paws. They looked as if they were trembling . . . until she realized that it was the ice underneath her that was moving. "What—" she started to say, but she was cut off by a rumbling, crashing noise from outside the den.

All three bears exchanged alarmed glances. The ice was vibrating furiously now. Kallik slipped as she jumped up and scrambled toward the entrance. The other two followed her as she pushed her way into the open air. The fog was a little thinner, but she couldn't see the source of the loud noise.

"What is it?" she shouted to Ujurak.

"I don't know!" he yelped.

Horror flooded through Kallik. It sounded a lot like the roar of a firebeast—along with a crashing and cracking that she'd never heard before, as if an entire forest were falling down around them.

"Run!" Ujurak roared. "We have to run! Now!"

CHAPTER NINETEEN

Ujurak

Ujurak's fur stood on end.

"You have to run!" he heard Kallik shouting at Iniq. The smaller white bear bundled into Iniq's side, shoving her away from the den and the approaching sound.

"I can't!" Iniq cried. "My legs won't carry me!" She stumbled weakly in the snow.

"You have to!" Ujurak bellowed. "It isn't safe!"

"RUN!" Kallik shouted again, snapping her teeth at Iniq's paws.

"My den!" Iniq wailed. She looked back over her shoulder as they pushed her forward. "My cubs!"

"Your cubs will grow up safely somewhere else!" Kallik insisted. "But not if you don't get out of here!"

Finally Iniq's paws seemed to start working again, and she scrambled along beside them as they ran. Ujurak gazed blindly into the mist. Where should they run to? Was anywhere safe? He couldn't even tell which direction the noise was coming from.

"Not that way!" Kallik barked, skidding to a halt. "It's getting louder over there!" She drove Iniq around and started running again, bolting away from the rumbling in the ice.

Ujurak ran until the ice stopped shaking beneath his paws, and then he slid to a halt, scattering snow around him. Kallik and Iniq stopped a few bearlengths away. They all looked back, gasping for air.

Out of the gloomy, horrible-smelling, reddish-brown mist slid a massive firebeast unlike any Ujurak had ever seen before. At first he thought it must be sliding across the ice, but when he looked closer, he realized that it was floating in the water and smashing the ice in front of it to get through. Its sharply pointed front end forced a path through by riding up and over the ice, then crushing and breaking the sheet with its own weight. Behind the firebeast was a narrow lane of open blue water edged with jagged pieces of ice.

Kallik gasped. Her claws sank into the snow, and Ujurak could see her shoulders shaking with fear. He could imagine how she felt—the ice seemed so solid, so firm beneath their feet. It was horrifying to realize there were firebeasts that could smash through her world so easily.

"The spirits," she whispered. Kallik believed the spirits of dead bears lived in the ice below them as well as in the stars. So this was even worse—a violation of the spirits' home, destroying Kallik's ancestors and protectors along with the ground she stood on.

The terrible grinding noise of the firebeast roared across the ice, nearly deafening them. Ujurak could smell the firebeast clearly now, too, its scent sharper and smokier than the red-brown mist. The mist was finally beginning to lift, and in the distance he spotted another firebeast following the first one. It was laden with blue and red cubes, and it trailed along the path the first ship had made.

Ujurak padded up to Kallik and leaned against her, trying to be comforting.

"That beast is stronger than the ice," Kallik whimpered, her voice shaking. "I didn't know anything like that existed." Beside her, Iniq crouched low to the ground. Her expression was equally terrified.

"It may seem that way," Ujurak said. "But remember, the ice always returns. Every snow-sky, there it is again, no matter how many firebeasts try to smash it down."

"I hope so," Kallik said softly.

"I can't use that den now," Iniq said. She nodded at the drift of snow in the distance. "It's too close to the path of the firebeast. And it was so beautiful!" She buried her nose in Kallik's fur.

"I'm sorry, I didn't know," Kallik said. "I've never seen a firebeast like that."

"I have," Iniq said with a shudder. "The no-claws and their firebeasts come here more and more to open up paths of water through the ice. Their noise and stench have made me move on before." She sighed. "I need to find somewhere safe for my cubs to be born, far away from the firebeasts."

Ujurak saw the sad look on Kallik's face. He knew she wanted to help. He wanted this bear and her cubs to be safe, too. He guessed that Kallik was also trying to replace Lusa—without realizing it, she was looking for another friend to save. But they didn't have time to wander the ice searching for a safe home for every bear. They had to keep moving. Couldn't Kallik understand that their mission was more important than one bear? That if they succeeded, it would help save *all* bears?

Suddenly Kallik lifted her head. "I think I smell seal," she said, inhaling deeply. "I'm going to check. I'll be right back." She padded away, sniffing intently.

Iniq lay down in the snow and rested her head on her paws. "You're lucky to have each other," she said. "I've always loved being on my own. But now, knowing that I'll soon have cubs depending on me—it all seems so much harder, somehow. Especially with the firebeasts everywhere. How can I bring cubs into a world like this?"

"Maybe it won't always be like this," Ujurak said. He wished he had his mother's strength and wisdom. If she were here, she'd know exactly what to say.

It wasn't long before Kallik came back, dragging a seal carcass. Her jaws were stained red. She dropped it at Iniq's paws. "This is for you and your cubs," she said. "I wish we could do more to help, but we have to keep going."

Ujurak met Kallik's gaze and nodded, glad that she understood.

Iniq's eyes widened at the fat seal flopped across her paws. "I haven't had seal in days!" she said. She gave them a sideways look as if she expected them to take it away from her again, and Kallik nodded reassuringly. Iniq tore hungrily into the newkill. Ujurak thought she might be hungrier than he had ever been in his life.

"Good-bye," Kallik said softly, backing away from Iniq. "May Silaluk watch over you."

Iniq didn't seem to have heard. Her claws ripped into the seal flesh as she wolfed it down.

Ujurak and Kallik turned toward the sun and began to walk again. Ujurak was trying to figure out how to tell Kallik that she'd done a good thing by giving Iniq some hope. But after half a skylength, Kallik turned to him with her normally gentle eyes blazing.

"How can it be like this?" she demanded. "Why should the no-claws destroy the ice? It isn't fair!"

"We're going to stop them," Ujurak reminded her. "That's what we're trying to do."

Kallik shook her head. "I don't see how," she muttered.

He couldn't imagine how, either. All he knew was that they had to keep going. His mother was waiting, and somewhere out there, he'd find a way to save the wild.

He had to.

CHAPTER TWENTY

Toklo

The reddish mist still hung over the ice, making Toklo's fur feel sticky and heavy. They had walked for most of the day without finding anything to eat, and Toklo couldn't smell anything except the haze.

He lifted his head as a cool breeze parted the mist for a brief moment, ruffling his fur. He squinted. There was something dark on the edge of the sky—something that wasn't just more white snow and ice. His heart leaped.

"Lusa!" he barked. "Do you see that? Tell me I'm not imagining it!"

Next to him, Lusa stood up on her back paws and peered through the haze. "What do you think it is?" she asked.

"Land!" he said. "Isn't it? It must be. Look how close we are!"

Lusa's ears twitched. "Maybe," she said. "I hear something . . . like a rumbling or a grinding. Could it be coming from the land?"

Toklo couldn't hear anything. "I'll be able to tell when we

get closer," he said. His paws felt lighter as he started walking again, speeding up to a trot. "Come on—maybe we'll even be able to sleep on land tonight!"

As they galloped across the snow, slipping on bare patches of ice, Toklo strained his ears to catch what Lusa had picked up. After a while he began to hear it. It sounded like a low grumbling, like a giant bear muttering to himself. And they were definitely heading toward it.

Lusa gave him an anxious glance. "Are you sure this is safe?" she panted. "A noise like that makes me think maybe we should run away."

"It's probably firebeasts," Toklo pointed out, although his fur tingled. "You know how their roaring carries. And if it is, that means they're on the land, and we're going the right way." He bumped her side. "We'll go around them when we get there. Don't worry about it."

Suddenly Lusa skidded to a stop. "Oh, no!" she cried. "Toklo, look!"

The flat, smooth snow they'd been running across ended after a few more bearlengths. After that, the ice was broken into large chunks, drifting on a dark, frozen river.

The two bears stood at the edge of the ice, looking down into the rippling darkness. Uneasiness prickled through Toklo's fur. He didn't want to swim again—to risk orcas, drowning, and being trapped under the ice. But it looked as though they didn't have a choice. The land he'd seen was hidden again by the haze, but he knew it was ahead of them.

"This makes sense," he said, trying to sound confident for

Lusa. "Remember, the ice was all broken up around the land. It must mean we're near the shore, that's all. We won't have to swim far before we get there."

"Really?" Lusa asked, dipping one paw into the water. She pulled it out and licked it, then shivered. "*Blech*. This water tastes horrible. Not just salty, but worse, somehow, like fire-beasts." She pawed at her tongue.

"Well, the plan is to swim in it, not drink it!" Toklo pointed out. Lusa made a face at him. "Let's go now, while it's still light enough to see." *Light enough to watch for orcas,* he thought. His eyes scanned the water for black fins, but he didn't see any signs of them.

Taking a deep breath, he slipped into the water and let out a yelp as the bone-chilling cold soaked into his fur. A quiet splash and another yelp told him that Lusa was right behind him. She surged up alongside him and they began to paddle with their paws, trying to keep their noses above the water. A wave swamped some of the seawater into Toklo's mouth and he spat, disgusted. Lusa was right—this water was worse than the salty seawater they'd swum in before. It tasted of firebeasts and black stuff and smoke.

It's because we're near the shore, he told himself again. *That's where most of the firebeasts are, so of course they've made the water taste like this.* But he felt a nagging doubt as he searched the sea for orcas, and he hoped that there were some bear spirits—white or brown—around to help guide them to the land.

A large blue chunk of ice bobbed in front of them, and they swam toward it gratefully. Lusa sank her claws into the side and Toklo gave her a boost to help her up. He heaved himself onto the ice and they sat, panting, for a few moments. The ice chunk was a few bearlengths long, with jagged edges as if it had been violently hacked away from the rest of the ice.

"Oh, look," Lusa said, scrambling to her paws. She padded over to the far side of the ice chunk and Toklo realized there was something small lying there. Lusa prodded it with one claw.

He padded over to join her. "It's a bird!" he said in surprise.

It looked like the gray and white birds that were always screaming annoyingly along the shore. This one was definitely dead.

Lusa poked it again. "Do you think we can eat it?"

Toklo sniffed it and wrinkled his nose. "It smells sort of nasty in a flat-face way, but I think it's still newkill, not rotfood." His stomach rumbled. "I guess we can," he said.

He set one paw on the bird's head and reached to claw off a chunk of flesh. But his paw sank into something sticky, and he pulled it away again quickly, only to discover that it was covered in the horrible black liquid that Ujurak had called "oil."

"Ew!" Lusa said. She sniffed his paw, then gingerly lifted the bird's wing with one claw. Its feathers were drenched in oil, covering it from beak to talons. It slithered a pawlength on the ice as Lusa poked it.

"We definitely can't eat that," Toklo said. He scraped at the top of the ice and tried to wash the sticky oil off his paw.

"How did it get that way?" Lusa asked in a hushed voice.

"I have no idea." Toklo was about to suggest swimming again when he heard a roar building from the distance, vibrating through the air. It sounded like something approaching. He whirled around and saw a giant floating firebeast snarling toward them through a channel it was making in the ice. It didn't even seem to notice the blocks of ice in its way; it smashed right through them as if they were ants.

Toklo and Lusa watched, puzzled, as the firebeast churned right past their chunk of ice. The huge wave that swelled up in its wake made the chunk tilt and dip and jump until they were thrown off into the water. More broken pieces of ice bobbed around them, whacking into their sides and spinning them as they were trying to swim. Toklo flailed his paws, frantically scanning the haze. He couldn't let himself be turned around too much. How far away was the land?

A dark shadow loomed through the reddish haze. It seemed surprisingly tall for something on a beach, but Toklo wasn't about to argue. He nudged Lusa toward it and they paddled as fast as they could, trying to dodge the bear-sized pieces of ice that drifted past. When he felt his paws getting tired, Toklo grabbed the nearest block of ice and called for Lusa to do the same. It was too small for them to climb onto, but it gave them a chance to breathe and rest their paws as they drifted across the river.

The dark shadow loomed closer and closer, and the haze became thinner. Toklo felt his paws bump into a thick shelf of ice. He'd been so busy watching the shadow, he hadn't realized they'd made it across the channel of water. Quickly he scrambled out into the biting wind and reached down to help Lusa up behind him.

Soaking wet, they huddled together, shivering and staring as the shadow became clearer.

"It's not land," Lusa said mournfully.

Toklo's heart sank. Instead of the trees and grass and mountains he'd hoped to see, they were looking at another terrifying flat-face construction. It rose up out of the water, twice as high as most flat-face dens, with dark metal legs. The rumbling and grinding came from its belly, and it was swarming with flat-faces.

It looked like the towers Toklo had seen on the islands as they swam across the Great River, or the ones around the denning place where they'd rescued Ujurak, by the nest of metal birds.

They weren't anywhere near the land. Toklo felt his hopes vanish. He'd wanted to lead Lusa to safety—but he'd only brought her to yet another terrible danger.

CHAPTER TWENTY-ONE

Lusa

Lusa's paws felt as if they were frozen to the ice. She'd never been so thoroughly wet and miserable before. She missed Kallik and Ujurak, and she was hungry again after swimming so far, and most of all, she wanted to *sleep*.

She heard Toklo take a deep breath beside her. "The land must be on the other side," he said. "So we'll go around it. Maybe we'll be able to see the shore from there."

It was strange to have Toklo being the one who stayed positive and encouraged her to keep going, but Lusa was glad that he was trying so hard to do that for her. She didn't have the energy to do it herself. The spark of hope that usually flared deep in her chest seemed to have faded to a dim ember, when she could find it at all. Even the memory of Arcturus the starbear talking to her couldn't revive her spirits; thinking about his confusing message only muddled her thoughts even more.

They crept closer to the dark tower across grayish snow that smelled of smoke. The reddish haze was thinner here, but mingled with a gritty taste in the air. Lusa's eyes stung and watered, making it hard to see the flat-faces clambering around the legs of the tower. Many of them were on floating firebeasts, peering into the water. Some of the firebeasts were small and roared grumpily as the flat-faces steered them quickly between the pieces of broken ice.

Lusa realized that the water around the dark tower was black and slimy. More black stuff was spurting out of a hole in the tower, although flat-faces in bright yellow pelts were gathered around it trying to plug it up. She saw a bird like the one they'd found dead, only this one was still alive. It was trapped in the black water, flapping its wings in a sickly way as it tried to launch itself into the sky.

"That stuff could kill all the birds around here, just like the one we found," she whispered to Toklo. "Look how far across the water it stretches. It's like it could cover the whole world."

Toklo glanced at the gray sky, which was getting darker by the moment. They couldn't see the sun clearly through the foggy haze, but Lusa guessed that it was setting, and that soon it would be night. She knew Toklo didn't want to sleep near the dark tower any more than she did. But if they tried to press on in the dark, one of them might slip and fall into that water—and end up just like the bird.

"There must be clearer water beyond the tower," Toklo said. "We just have to get there. Can you go faster?"

Lusa nodded, although her paws ached and her legs felt like useless tree stumps that were about to fall off. She forced herself to run as Toklo took off across the ice. They kept the tower to their left, hoping to find a way around it on the other side.

But they were only level with the center of the construction when they heard flat-face voices yelling, much closer than the ones around the tower. Lusa bundled into Toklo as he skidded to a stop. Her fur stood on end at the terrified look on his face.

"Flat-faces!" he cried. "With firesticks!"

She saw four flat-faces running toward them across the snow. They had clearly spotted the bear cubs; they were pointing at the bears and shouting to one another. Lusa's memory swooped back to the hunters on Smoke Mountain, chasing them across the moonlit meadow before capturing Toklo and taking him away in their firebeast.

They turned to run back the way they'd come, but more flat-faces were on the river now, standing on their floating firebeasts as they swarmed around the tower. They'd never get back across the river without being spotted.

Lusa spun in place, her heart pounding as she stared at the flat-faces that surrounded them. "Toklo! What do we do?"

"Into the water," he ordered, shoving her toward the black, sticky mess around the tower legs.

"But—the bird—" Lusa protested.

"We don't have a choice! Just swim and keep swimming, and don't get it on your muzzle," Toklo growled. Lusa's paws pounded across the ice as they ran toward the water. The flat-faces were still chasing them, but on foot the bears were much faster.

Then again, she knew from past experience that the pellets from their firesticks moved fastest of all. Lusa expected to hear the crack of a firestick at any moment, which made her run even faster.

Toklo didn't even stop to scan the water as they reached the edge. He lifted his head and jumped right in. Black stuff splattered up on the ice around Lusa's paws. She looked back at the running flat-faces, took a deep breath, and leaped in after Toklo.

It was horrible in the water, sticky and hard to swim and chokingly revolting. Her paws moved slowly, as if they were wrapped in honey—but the most foul-tasting, foul-smelling honey in the world. Lusa's fur instantly clogged up with black stuff, weighing her down. It was hard to paddle, harder still to keep her snout above the water. She wanted to call to Toklo for help, but she couldn't open her mouth, or the oil would spill in and choke her. She was having trouble breathing with the black stuff so close to her nose.

She summoned all her strength and swam as hard as she could. If they could make it past the tower, into the water beyond, they should be able to find more ice and somewhere to rest while they hid from the flat-faces. She wished she knew how far they had to swim, but it was impossible to see beyond the tower. It was difficult even to see Toklo paddling a bear-length ahead of her.

Suddenly she felt a sharp pain in her rump. Fighting back a yelp of surprise, Lusa twisted around and saw something thin and pointy sticking out of her fur. For a moment she thought it was a giant bee stinger, but then she realized that bees had more sense than to venture out onto the ice.

More sense than me, she thought woozily. Black bear in a white bear world. *Why are my paws so heavy?*

Something like a thick spiderweb dropped over her head. She batted at it with her claws, but all her movements were suddenly slower and weaker than they should be. The web closed around her, dragging her through the water. Lusa stopped fighting and clung to the strands at the top. It took all her concentration just to keep her head above the water as she was pulled along.

"Lusa!" she heard someone yell. "Lusa! Lusa!"

Sounds like Toklo, she thought. *Here I am, Toklo.* Had she actually called back to him? She wasn't sure. She was so *tired.* Was this the longsleep? Had it finally won—now, in the middle of the black sea while they were being chased by flat-faces? *That's rather inconvenient,* she thought, and then her eyes drifted shut.

She forced her eyes open again as she was pulled onto a floating firebeast the color of leaves. Flat-faces reached their pale, clawless paws toward her, but instead of fighting back or trying to escape . . . she fell asleep.

CHAPTER TWENTY-TWO

Ujurak

The red mist had finally lifted, and the sun shone hazily on the jagged peaks and cliffs of ice all around Ujurak and Kallik.

Ujurak glanced at Kallik, who was trudging along silently beside him. He knew she was missing Lusa and Toklo—he missed them, too. Their absence left an aching hollow feeling inside him. All the confidence he'd found in the meeting with his mother was ebbing away. If he was doing the right thing, walking toward the rising sun, why did he feel so lost?

A breeze ruffled his thick brown fur and he shivered at the chill in the air. It was just after sunhigh, but the sun was hidden by thin gray clouds, so not much warmth filtered down to Ujurak's skin. His claws dug into the snow as they worked their way up a long white slope. Solid blocks of blue-gray ice loomed on either side of them, and he could smell the salty tang of the sea close by.

They came over the crest of the slope and the snow abruptly turned to slick ice below their paws, so that Ujurak slipped and tumbled down the hill toward an open slash of water, and even Kallik stumbled after him, having trouble keeping her footing.

Ujurak skidded to an ungainly stop at the bottom and realized with a start that there was a large brown shape flopped on the edge of the ice, a few bearlengths in front of them.

"RAAARRRGH!" the creature bellowed, spotting them. Kallik stopped helping Ujurak to his paws and whipped around to face it. Ujurak could see that her whole body was shaking with fear.

The large brown animal charging toward them didn't exactly have legs; it hauled itself forward on huge, flat feet, but it still moved shockingly fast. It was long and wrinkled, like a giant slug or caterpillar. Its face was squashed and whiskery, with two enormous pointed teeth sticking down out of its mouth.

"A walrus!" Kallik gasped. "Ujurak, run!" She shoved him behind her and reared up on her hind legs, slashing her claws in the air to look threatening. She let out a roar, but Ujurak could hear the wobbly note in her voice that said she was terrified. He remembered the "Walrus Attack" game she'd played with Lusa; walruses must be one of the very few things that scared white bears, and if it was bad enough to scare Kallik, it definitely scared him.

The walrus lunged at Kallik with its mouth open and she thumped it in the head with one of her massive paws, knocking it aside. Its tusks skimmed her fur and she dodged away as it charged again. Ujurak realized that she was trying to draw it away from him. But he couldn't stand by and watch her be gored by those horrible long teeth. He charged up behind the walrus and sank his teeth into the tough, greasy hide of its back. The taste on his tongue was slimy and salty all at once.

The walrus roared and spun toward him, swiping its tusks dangerously close to his face. Ujurak jumped away and darted in a circle around it as Kallik did the same, each of them pulling the creature's attention in a different direction. It roared again, a deep, furious bellow that echoed across the ice.

Ujurak felt a strange prickling under his fur. He looked down and saw his paws getting bigger. White fur was starting to peek out between the brown tufts. He was turning into a white bear! His body must instinctively know that a white bear was a more powerful animal for fighting a walrus.

No! his mind cried. *I won't change again!* A part of him sensed that his mother wouldn't mind—that she approved of his power. But a bigger part of him remembered how he lost himself as a goose and then as a whale, and he was terrified of his real self disappearing forever.

He concentrated his energy on thinking about brown bears. Brown, shaggy fur, hunched shoulders, swaying gait. *Brown bear!* To his satisfaction, the white fur retreated back into his skin and his paws shrank back down. He was himself again.

"Ujurak!" Kallik screamed.

Ujurak threw himself to the ground and rolled away just in time as the walrus sensed his distraction and attacked. Bellowing, the walrus tried to wriggle after him. Ujurak felt his back pressed up against a snowbank. There was nowhere to run. The walrus and its gleaming tusks were nearly upon him.

Suddenly Kallik reared up behind the walrus and plunged her long, sharp claws into its neck. She bit down hard and blood sprayed across the snow. The walrus thrashed and roared in pain, but Ujurak scrambled over its back to pin its tail down. The rubbery muscle heaved underneath him and he had to sink his claws in and throw all his weight on it. Gradually the thrashing stopped. The blood slowed to a trickle, and the walrus flopped over, its tiny eyes staring blankly at the gray sky.

Kallik stepped back, panting. Blood was smeared across the white fur around her mouth and Ujurak could see patches of red from tiny cuts on her body. His front shoulder ached where the walrus had walloped him, but he didn't sense any more serious injuries. He followed Kallik over to a snowbank, limping from his bruised shoulder, and they both rolled in the fresh white snow until they felt clean again. He let his paws droop in the snow and lay there, catching his breath.

That was far too close. He had done his best, and Kallik had been amazing, but the truth was that the walrus would never have dared to attack them if Toklo and Lusa had been with them as well. What were they supposed to do if a fully grown white bear decided to pick a fight with them? More important, how were Toklo and Lusa supposed to defend themselves without him and Kallik there to help?

We never should have split up, he thought, his heart sinking. *That was a terrible mistake.* He looked at the dead walrus, then followed its empty gaze up to the sky. Piles of dark clouds huddled low on the horizon, while thinner gray clouds overhead drifted slowly across the weak sun.

Something appeared against the backdrop of the sky, and Ujurak squinted. It looked like a thin white streak . . . no, it was *four* thin white streaks! They slashed across the sky, as if an invisible claw were painting them there. Then, as he watched, they crossed toward one another and merged, creating one long, fat white streak that disappeared behind the darkest clouds in the distance.

Four into one. Four bears completing a journey together. That was how it was supposed to be.

"Come eat some walrus." Kallik broke into his thoughts, nudging him with her cold black nose. "It might be gross, but at least it's food."

Ujurak staggered to his paws and followed her to the carcass of the walrus. Kallik used her claws to slice open its thick, wrinkled brown skin and they both dug into the meat inside. It was greasy and foul tasting, with a strong hint of fish and ocean water, and far more blubber than meat. But Ujurak hadn't realized how hungry he was; at least it restored his strength.

They left the rest of the walrus carcass and kept walking, skirting the edge of the sea and the dark water lapping at the ice near them. Ujurak couldn't stop thinking about Toklo and Lusa. Four bears together were stronger than two.

"What's that?" Kallik interrupted his thoughts again. She nodded at something small on the ice ahead of them.

Ujurak looked and felt a shiver through his fur. He didn't

know what it was yet, but he could see a gray and black and white lump, lying still on the ice.

They padded closer and saw that the lump was a dead seabird with its claws curled up in the air and its wings frozen solid. Its beak was slightly open and its beady eyes were empty. Streaks of black oil matted its gray and white feathers.

Ujurak stared down at the dead bird with a feeling of dread.

"Come on," Kallik said, nudging him gently. "It's getting dark. Let's find somewhere to sleep." She sniffed the bird. "I hope you're not hungry, because I wouldn't eat this. It smells bad, and not just in a rotfood kind of way."

Ujurak shook his head. He couldn't have eaten anything. The walrus meat was still filling his belly, and his thoughts were a whirl of guilt and worry. Where were Toklo and Lusa? If he and Kallik were weaker without them, how much weaker would those two be without any guidance on the ice? He should never have let them go alone.

They walked farther along the sea edge until they couldn't see or smell the bird anymore—or at least, Ujurak couldn't. He wondered if Kallik's powerful nose still could, but she didn't mention it. She dug a half cave out of a snowbank and they both curled into it, protected from the cool wind blowing softly across the ice.

As darkness swept across the sky, Kallik fell asleep with her head on her paws. Ujurak stared out to sea. He was too restless and anxious to sleep, although his muscles were all tired from walking so far. Was he doing the wrong thing? He looked up at the stars that were beginning to crowd the sky. There were so many of them! But he had no trouble finding the constellation that was his mother.

Please help me, he thought. *Please tell me what to do. Is this the wrong thing? It was all so clear before. But without Toklo and Lusa . . . I don't know what's right anymore.*

Kallik whimpered in her sleep. Ujurak huddled a little closer to her, hoping the warmth of his fur would comfort her in whatever dream she was having.

A light caught his attention—a small, twinkling light, like a star, but low in the sky, close to the water. He stared at it for a moment, then jumped a little as a second light joined it. The two tiny lights blinked next to each other for a moment. Then a third appeared . . . and a fourth.

Four lights, Ujurak thought with a shiver. They blinked in a regular pattern, not like the constant shining of the stars.

All at once, two of them went out. Only two were left, blinking slower . . . and slower . . . and then they faded out as well.

That was it. Ujurak couldn't ignore the signs. They had to go back and find Toklo and Lusa. Whatever happened after that would happen. But they were four bears traveling the claw path, and they had to complete that journey together.

As he had that thought, the green and blue fire flared in the sky above him. The bear spirits were dancing again. Surely that meant they approved of his decision.

"Kallik," he said, nudging her in the side. "Kallik, wake up."

The white bear started awake with a cry of distress. She sat up and stared around wildly for a moment as though she'd forgotten where she was. Finally she turned to Ujurak with wide eyes.

"I had the most awful dream," she said. "It was Silaluk—she was being shot with arrows by the hunters." Ujurak shifted uneasily. "And she was crying out with pain," Kallik went on. "But Ujurak . . . she sounded like Lusa!"

"Lusa?" Ujurak echoed. "Is she hurt?"

Kallik shook her head. "It was just a dream." She pawed at her face. "I'm sorry, it scared me. It was only a bad dream." She blinked, trying to look cheerful again. "That'll teach me to eat walrus meat."

"It might not be just a dream," Ujurak said. His pelt prickled with fear. What if he was already too late? "I've made up my mind. We're going back to find Toklo and Lusa."

CHAPTER TWENTY-THREE

Toklo

"Lusa!" Toklo shouted again. The small black bundle of wet fur that was his friend was being hauled up the side of the floating firebeast. Toklo paddled frantically toward it, but she disappeared over the side before he was halfway there. He could see flat-faces in brightly colored skins gathering around Lusa. What were they going to do to her?

Another floating firebeast came roaring around the side of the tower, spraying water and black smoke on either side of it as it charged between him and the firebeast where Lusa was being held captive. The flat-faces hadn't spotted him yet, but Toklo knew he had only a moment to escape before they did.

He hesitated, his fur prickling with fear and anguish. If he climbed onto the firebeast, perhaps he could fight off all the flat-faces and save Lusa. But he'd never be able to drag her through this sticky water without help, and it wouldn't do any good to rescue her if he just went ahead and drowned her.

He'd have to hope the flat-faces kept her alive, and then he could rescue her later. In which case *he* needed to stay out of their paws as well.

Toklo swam for the nearest ice, several bearlengths from one of the tower legs. He climbed out onto the snow, and for the first time he appreciated how cold and clean it felt against his paws. He'd never thought he could be happier to be on snow than on dirt, but now he rolled and wriggled in it until his thick brown fur was soaking wet and the black stuff ran off him in gooey rivulets. He couldn't get it all off, but at least the streaks of black on his paws were less thick and sticky.

The high-pitched chatter of flat-face voices floated across the ice. Toklo pricked his ears. They were coming toward him! He whirled around and spotted a large snowdrift nearby. Quickly he dove into it and dug until he'd buried himself well inside, then he covered himself over with the snow. This was one useful thing Kallik had taught him about surviving on the ice.

Please don't smell me, he thought, listening to the flat-faces come closer and closer. Maybe the snow would hide his smell. He knew Kallik would have been able to find him easily, but flat-faces didn't smell as well as bears.

There were two of them, muttering to each other and stamping their feet as if they were trying to keep warm. Toklo wondered what they were talking about. Were they still looking for him? If they were trying to hunt, they were doing a great job of letting the prey know they were coming. For relatively small creatures, flat-faces made an awful lot of noise. *And mess,* he thought ruefully, burying one of his oil-stained paws deeper in the snow.

Well, if they weren't using their ears to hunt, they apparently weren't using their noses, either. The flat-faces went straight past his snowdrift without even pausing. The squeak and chatter of their voices grated on his ears. He wished he could paw the melting snow out of his eyes, but he was afraid to move in case they spotted him.

Toklo waited a long time, letting the cold snow seep into his fur, until he was sure they were long gone. Finally he pawed his way into the open again. The sun had completely set while he was hiding, and now the dark night sky arched overhead, speckled with glittering stars. He shook himself until droplets of melted snow and oil splattered around him.

Toklo lifted his head and breathed in deeply. It was hard to pick out any scents beyond the overwhelming smell of the oil that lingered on his fur and coated the water behind him. He kept very still and let the wind rush around him until, faintly, he caught a jumble of smells coming from somewhere to his right, where the flat-faces had gone.

Cautiously he crept in that direction, keeping himself low to the ice so he could dive into another pile of snow if he saw any more flat-faces or firebeasts. The activity on the water had slowed down, although a few firebeasts still trawled below the tower.

After he had padded for a short distance, he spotted something large that stood out darkly against the pale snow up ahead. It was the size of a flat-face den, but its edges rippled oddly in the night wind. It glowed from the inside with light like small fires. As he got closer, he realized that it was like the tiny dens they'd seen near Smoke Mountain, with the walls that he could slice right through with his claws. His hopes rose. If Lusa was in there, maybe it wouldn't be so hard to get in and save her.

He closed his eyes and sniffed the air. The jumble of scents began to separate into clear smells—more oil, but also birds and seals! Inside the flat-face den! He strained to distinguish one scent that made him think of leaves and cool streams and warm dirt. His heart leaped as he recognized it. It was Lusa! It had to be!

Toklo nearly bounced on his paws the way she did. She was alive! And he'd found her! Now he just had to get to her. He wondered if she could catch any of the birds or seals that were inside the den with her. Then at least she'd get something to eat. His stomach growled and his mouth watered at the thought of biting into a juicy bird or seal.

He crept as close as he dared to the den, only a few bear-lengths from its rippling walls. He could hear the murmur of flat-face voices inside, and a few firebeasts were sleeping outside, but it was quiet and still where he was. Toklo edged around the den, trying to find the spot where Lusa's scent was strongest. There were so many other smells mingled together; she must be surrounded by flat-faces. Perhaps this wasn't the best time to charge in and pick a fight.

His paws crunched on some rough snow and he paused as the voices inside surged upward. Had they heard him? He tried straining his ears to hear their muttering, but even the sounds he could catch meant nothing to him. One of the lights separated from the others and moved to the door. Toklo was near the back, so he couldn't tell if flat-faces came out of the front. He scrambled back a few bearlengths and stopped where he could see the den entrance.

Suddenly a bright fiery light whizzed into the sky. Toklo fell back on his hindquarters with a yelp of surprise. Another light shot up after it, and he heard flat-face voices shouting. They were throwing fire at him! He turned and bolted up the slope away from the den. He ran until the burning smell of the fire was far behind him.

Finally he stopped and looked back, panting. The bright lights were fizzing out, and the flat-faces had gone back inside the den. They weren't even chasing him. They were just trying to get rid of him!

Toklo was indignant. How dare they drive him away from Lusa? She was *his* friend! And she needed him! He growled and sank his claws into the snow, glaring down at the warm lights moving around inside the den. He had no choice. He had to back off and wait for a better chance, although it tore him up inside to leave Lusa even a moment longer in there. But tomorrow he'd find his way in, and then those flat-faces would be sorry!

Toklo stomped through the snow to a spot where he could dig out a shelter and keep an eye on the den in the distance. His cave wasn't as stable as the kind Kallik built, but he managed to pack snowy walls around himself enough to block the freezing wind. He turned in a circle a few times and lay down, resting his head on his paws. It seemed as though there were as many stars above him as hairs in his pelt.

He spotted the Pathway Star and sighed. It looked lonelier than ever tonight.

CHAPTER TWENTY-FOUR

Lusa

When Lusa woke up, she was lying on a table with a light as bright as the sun hanging over her. Something was in her fur, like large beetles crawling through it. She tried to sit up to see what it was, then realized that she was stuck to the table with thick brown vines. A small cage was tied over her mouth so she couldn't use her teeth to free herself.

Panic rose in her chest. What was happening? Where was she? She flailed her paws as much as she could, growling and struggling against the vines.

"Shhhh," said a flat-face voice by her head. Lusa felt strong, gentle paws stroke her fur between her ears. A memory flooded back of one of the keepers in the Bear Bowl, stroking her in just that way when Lusa was a tiny cub.

Lusa reluctantly lay still, trying to figure out what was going on. She realized that the insects crawling over her fur were actually flat-face paws. Their long, thin toes were deft and surprisingly gentle. They were washing the sticky stuff out of her fur!

She relaxed a little more. Perhaps these were the good kind of flat-faces, like the keepers in the Bear Bowl. Toklo might not believe they existed, but Lusa knew they did. She remembered the fruit they had brought her and the way they had healed her mother when she was sick. Maybe these flat-faces were trying to heal her as well, by cleaning her fur of the stuff that had killed the bird.

Her eyes had adjusted to the bright light by now, so she could see beyond it to a thin, dark green skin that stretched overhead and came down to form four walls around a big open space. The way it flapped and rippled reminded her of the little dens that they'd stolen food from in the woods, before Smoke Mountain, although this one was much, much bigger.

She saw that there were other tables and cages around her, plus lots and lots of flat-faces, all of them working and murmuring to one another and hurrying from one cage to the next. Lusa saw more of the gray-and-white birds, some of them crouching in tubs of clean water as the flat-faces cleaned their feathers. She also spotted three seals in cages, all of them looking tired and sad and sticky.

There was an animal she didn't recognize in one of the cages. It was huge and fat and blubbery, like a giant wrinkly seal, but with whiskers and two huge, pointy teeth sticking out of its mouth. Lusa would have been frightened, but it looked so sick, she thought she could probably climb all over it without its even reacting to her.

She twisted her head to look up at the flat-face faces around her. They seemed kind and careful, cleaning her fur without pulling on it or hurting her. Why were they doing this? Lusa couldn't understand. Why would flat-faces pour the black sticky stuff into the water, then run around and gather up all the animals it touched and clean them off? Why not leave the black stuff out of the water in the first place? It made Lusa's head hurt to think about it.

"I don't get it," one of the flat-faces said in the chirrupy, high-pitched voice they all had. "I keep cleaning and cleaning this patch of fur, and it just stays black."

Lusa couldn't understand what they were saying, but this one sounded puzzled.

"Same here!" said another.

"I don't think it is a polar bear cub after all," said the one at her head. "Look at these enormous ears. I think it's a black bear cub."

Lusa nudged his paw with her nose. She wanted him to go back to stroking her fur instead of tapping her ears for whatever reason.

"All the way out here?" said the first. Her chirpy voice went up and up.

Lusa felt herself drifting into sleep again. The gentle fingers in her fur were soothing, and she felt like a cub being nuzzled by her mother and denmates. It was warm here, perhaps even safe, and at least she didn't have to swim or run or worry about—

Toklo!

She struggled to wake up again. She couldn't believe she'd forgotten about her friend, even for a moment. Was he in the den with her? Was he in one of the cages? Had the flat-faces captured him, too . . . or was he still out there, swimming through the poisonous black water?

But although she fought to open her eyes, the powerful pull of her exhaustion won out, and sleep crept over her. One question echoed through her mind just before darkness took over.

Where is Toklo?

CHAPTER TWENTY-FIVE

Toklo

When Toklo opened his eyes again, it was late morning. The sun was creeping up the sky, burning away the last gray clouds.

Toklo yawned and stretched his stiff, cold legs. He stared across the snow peaks at the flappy den. Flat-faces were swarming around it, going in and out of the front or roaring away on firebeasts and roaring back again. It was far too busy to go anywhere near it. Disgruntled, he flopped down again and stared at the den, trying to form a plan. He'd have to approach at night, when it was quieter . . . and this time he'd sneak up so silently they'd never hear him coming.

It was a long, cold day, and his worry about Lusa grew and grew as he watched the flat-faces. They moved so quickly and chattered so loud. What were they doing to her in there? Did she have food? What if she fell asleep and they didn't know to wake her up? He imagined bursting into the den and finding her in the longsleep, impossible to move or awaken. A shudder rippled through his pelt.

His stomach ached with hunger, but he couldn't tear

himself away from his post long enough to search for prey. He waited as the sun marched slowly across the sky. At least it was getting dark a lot sooner now, although the flat-faces barely seemed to notice. They produced light from things in their paws and kept scurrying around in the same frantic way.

Finally it looked as though most of the firebeasts had fallen asleep, and only one or two flat-faces were moving around the outside of the den. Toklo got up and started padding toward them. His fur prickled impatiently and his claws itched to slash at something. He was ready to pick a fight with the flat-faces if they tried to scare him off again.

He was only halfway there when an enormous firebeast came roaring up with its eyes blazing beams of light directly into the den. Several big flat-faces with furry chins and black, rubbery pelts jumped off the firebeast. They were shouting and waving their forelegs around.

More flat-faces came hurrying out of the den. All of them started shouting as well. Toklo skidded to a stop. Dismayed, he watched the flat-faces arguing. Several of them pointed at the dark tower. They all sounded very angry.

He sat down to wait. The ice was cold against his hind-quarters, but his attention was focused on the den. One of the flat-faces ran inside and carried out a small cage. Inside was a seabird, lolling sickly against the silvery webbed walls. Even from where he sat, Toklo could smell the black stuff and see it coating the bird's feathers. The flat-face pointed at the bird and shouted even louder, but the new flat-faces on the enormous firebeast only snorted and waved their hands as if the bird didn't interest them.

It interested Toklo, though. He realized that Lusa must also be inside a cage in the den. He felt quite silly for not thinking of that sooner. Of course she couldn't just be wandering around in there; the flat-faces wouldn't allow that. And if she were free to move around, she'd walk straight out the door to find him—he knew she would.

But if she was inside a cage, he'd need even more time to free her than he'd thought. He couldn't just burst in there, waving his claws around and roaring, and run off with her. He'd have to spend time figuring out how to open the cage first. Which meant he needed a more stealthy approach. Toklo looked at the shouting flat-faces again and sighed. Flat-faces liked shouting so much, this could go on all night. He needed to retreat and think of a new plan.

As he trekked back to his makeshift den, his paws kept slipping on the treacherous ice. At night it was harder to figure out the best places to walk. The second time he fell, his front paws skidded out to either side and he banged his chin hard on the ice. Wincing with pain, he got up and crept even more slowly across the snow.

If only they were back on land! He was sure he'd be able to rescue Lusa much more easily if they were surrounded by dirt and trees and grass, like they should be. And there would be prey everywhere! His stomach growled again, but he was too tired and his chin hurt too much for him to try hunting.

He curled up in his snow den and dozed restlessly. His dreams were muddled and harrowing, with flat-faces chasing him through endless ice and other flat-faces popping out from the snow just to yell in their high-pitched, nonsensical way. The smell of oil filled his nose, and as he ran, the black stuff seeped out of the snow and stuck to his paws, no matter how much he tried to wipe it off again.

When he woke up again, his head was aching. The sky was starting to lighten, a pale line of honey-colored fur glowing on the edge of the sky.

He had the strange feeling that something had woken him. A sound, perhaps—and then it came again. Scuffling and crunching on the snow. Someone was coming toward him! He took in a deep breath and recognized the musty, furry scent of bears.

Growling, Toklo leaped to his paws and burst out of the snow. He bared his teeth, ready to fight off any white bear, no matter how big it was.

But to his shock, the first face he saw belonged to a brown bear, who stared back at him with equally startled dark eyes. And then, finally, he recognized the scents.

"Ujurak!" Toklo gasped. He spotted the white bear behind his shape-shifting friend. "Kallik!"

"Toklo!" Ujurak barked. He peered around and then gave Toklo a worried look.

Toklo didn't know what to say. *Yes, I lost Lusa. I couldn't protect her or take her back to safety after all.* The weight of his guilt pressed down on his shoulders, and for a moment he couldn't speak.

"Oh, no," Kallik said, sniffing the air and looking horrified. "We were right. Something has happened to Lusa!"

CHAPTER TWENTY-SIX

Lusa

Lusa couldn't tell whether it was day or night inside the flat-face den. There were lights around her and above her when she opened her eyes, and she saw flat-faces awake and moving around through the cages.

But she thought it was dawn when she woke up for real the second time. The green walls of the den seemed paler, as if sunlight was trying to sneak through from the other side. Lusa sat up in her cage, rubbing her eyes with her paws. She felt much more alert than she had the day before. And she was very hungry.

She peered out through the bars and realized that she wasn't the only one who was hungry. A seal flopped in a cage only a few bearlengths from her, barking pitifully. Seabirds were squawking and flapping their wings in cages all over the den. She could hear whimpers and growls that sounded unfamiliar; she couldn't even guess what animals they might be coming from.

To her surprise, as she looked around, she spotted another

bear! He must have been brought in during the night, while she was asleep. She edged closer to the bars to peer at him. His cage was much bigger than hers, because he was a full-sized white bear. He was still asleep—or unconscious—his chest rising and falling with a ragged snorting sound. She thought she should be afraid of him, but the truth was that he reminded her of Qopuk, the frail old bear they'd met not far from Great Bear Lake.

Like Qopuk, this bear looked too weak to stand on his own paws. Just in case, though, the flat-faces had tied him down securely, binding his paws together so he couldn't claw anyone. His fur was streaked with sticky black oil, although Lusa guessed that the flat-faces had already washed some of it off, as they had for her.

She wriggled around to sniff herself and check her pelt. It felt much cleaner and glossier than it had when she was first hauled out of the sticky, black-stained water. She could still smell the oil, but that scent was heavy in the air all the time, so she wasn't sure if it was lingering in her fur as well.

A clatter from a nearby cage caught her attention. She saw a flat-face pushing a silver bowl into the seal's cage. They were being fed! That meant food should be coming her way, too. She tried to stand on her hind paws to see better and bumped her head against the top of the cage.

A flat-face voice murmured something soothing above her, although Lusa had no idea what the words meant. A young female flat-face crouched beside her cage and used a stick to push a container in through a gap at the bottom.

Lusa rushed over and buried her nose in the bowl. To her enormous disappointment, it was filled with meaty, fatty brown stuff—not what she really wanted at all. She poked the bowl with her nose, scooting it along the floor of the cage. When she had it stuck in the corner, she tried to nibble at the meat, but it was so rich and heavy that her stomach churned before she could swallow her first mouthful. She pawed at her face, then sat down and looked up at the flat-face mournfully.

The female was standing there, watching her. She made a noise like "Hmmm," then called another flat-face over. They pointed at the meat in the bowl and chattered to each other for a moment. The second flat-face nodded and walked away.

A few moments passed, and Lusa began to lose hope. Maybe they were just watching her. Maybe they were only curious; maybe they didn't understand or care that she didn't want any meat right now. She sniffed at the meat again, but couldn't bring herself to eat any more.

Clang! Lusa jumped as a bowl collided with her cage. The second flat-face had returned, carrying a new bowl. She ducked and shoved it through the gap toward Lusa. Eagerly Lusa hurried over. *What now?*

It was fruit! Real fruit, although not the fresh kind she used to get in the Bear Bowl. This fruit tasted like the kind she and Toklo had found in the silver containers back on the giant floating firebeast. But that was still better than no fruit, and *much* better than meat! Lusa gobbled it up, slurping the last of the juice from the bottom of the bowl. She licked her

202 SEEKERS: FIRE IN THE SKY

lips and her paws, then gave the flat-faces a hopeful glance.

The younger one laughed and said something. The second one nodded and went off again. Lusa hoped she was going to get more fruit. Her instincts told her these were good flat-faces, and they still seemed to be acting like it. Cleaning up sick animals, feeding her fruit . . . those were kind things to do.

On the other hand, she was trapped in a cage. She paced around the narrow space, sniffing the bars anxiously. Surely they weren't going to keep her locked up for very long. Right?

But then . . . what *were* they planning to do with her?

CHAPTER TWENTY-SEVEN

Kallik

Kallik didn't know whether to be relieved or alarmed when she heard about Lusa being trapped inside the pelt-den with the no-claws. Lusa was in trouble, but at least she was probably still alive. Kallik turned her nose into the wind.

"I *knew* I could still smell her," she said. "But it's so faint—all muddled up with other scents."

The sun was stretching its long rays over the snow, warming Kallik's pelt and turning Ujurak and Toklo's brown fur golden. She could see the pelt-den Toklo was talking about, nearly a skylength away, over the peaks of snowdrifts in between.

"I tried to get inside," Toklo said, "but the flat-faces clearly don't want any bears around. Unless they've already caught them, I mean."

"Maybe that's what we should do!" Kallik suggested, standing up. Her paws itched to be doing *something*. Lusa needed their help! The cries of distress from her dream still rang in Kallik's ears. "Maybe if we let them catch us, we'll be able to fight our way out from the inside, with Lusa."

Toklo hunched his shoulders. "I don't want any flat-faces touching me," he muttered.

"But if it's the only way in—" Kallik started to say. She realized that Ujurak was shaking his head.

"It might be a way in," he said, "but it's not a good way out. The flat-faces will kill us if we hurt them, and trying to fight our way out of the pelt-den means we'd almost certainly have to hurt some of them."

"Yeah, Lusa would never agree to that," Toklo said. "She still thinks some of them are actually good." He snorted, shooting an angry glance at the tower in the distance.

Kallik wanted to argue about it, but she realized that they were both right. It wouldn't do any good if they got captured and weren't able to get out again. She sat down, frustration prickling through her pelt. Lusa was so close, and yet so far away.

"I wish I could just walk into that pelt-den and set her free," she sighed.

Suddenly she had an idea. Her fur tingled with excitement. She looked up and met Toklo's eyes. He looked as if he'd had the same thought. They both turned to Ujurak.

He had his head down, licking up some melted snow from his paws, so it took him a moment to realize they were both staring at him. He blinked, then rocked back on his hindquarters.

"What?" he asked. "What are you—don't even—"

"You *have* to," Kallik said. "It's the only way, Ujurak."

Toklo nodded.

"You have to turn into a no-claw," Kallik insisted. "Then you really *could* just walk in there and set her free."

"No!" Ujurak said, wriggling as if he was trying to plant himself deeper into the snow. "No, I'm a brown bear! That's what I am, and I'm going to stay that way!"

"Stop being a baby," Toklo growled. "You've been whining about this since I met you. I think it's a stupid power, too, but as long as you have it, you might as well use it when it can actually be helpful."

Ujurak looked offended. "You don't understand what it's like! It's much more complicated than—"

"Blah blah blah," Toklo interrupted him. He got up and stood nose to nose with Ujurak, snarling. "Oh, you're so tortured, it's so hard to be a shape-shifting bear, nobody understands you! Well, get over it. Do you honestly think that if there was anything I could do to get inside that den and free Lusa, that I wouldn't do it? No matter how 'complicated' it was?"

"Um," Kallik said, trying to edge between the two brown bears. The last thing they needed was a fight! Ujurak's claws were digging into the snow as though he was about to leap at Toklo's throat. She'd never seen him so angry before; it was a bit terrifying to see the little bear so furious.

"Wait, listen," she begged. "Ujurak! Your mother gave you your powers, didn't she? It's something she taught you about. She never told you not to do it. She believed in you. It's like your gift from her—the way Nisa taught me about hunting seals, or Oka taught Toklo about catching salmon."

Ujurak's fur settled across his shoulders, as if the thought of his mother calmed him down.

"So you can't just ignore your powers," Kallik went on, "or pretend they don't exist, because they do. And maybe they're an important part of what we're out here to do. Isn't that possible?"

Ujurak looked down at his paws. Toklo took a step back and gave Kallik a grudging nod of approval.

Encouraged, Kallik persevered, "Besides, it's for Lusa. And you said we need her to save the wild."

Toklo looked less pleased at this, but Ujurak was nodding. He sighed a long, deep sigh. "I guess you're right," he said. He gave Kallik a sideways, head-tilted look. "How'd you get so wise?"

"From listening to you yap all the time," she said, nudging him affectionately.

"I'm just worried," he admitted in a small voice. He clawed a pile of snow into a ball and began rolling it back and forth. "Sometimes when I'm in another shape, I forget who I really am. And I think it's getting worse. Last time I was a flat-face, I only remembered that I was really a bear because of those three little bears the healer gave me. What if I go into the pelt-den and forget why I'm there? What if I never become a bear again?"

Kallik shivered. She couldn't imagine giving up her bear life forever—especially if it meant replacing it with the body of a no-claw! They were so weak and furless. She'd hate having to live so close to firebeasts all the time, with their nasty burning smell. No, that wouldn't be fun at all.

"If you don't come back," Toklo growled, "then we'll come tearing through the walls and get you. *That* ought to remind you about bears!"

"Just think about your mother," Kallik added quickly. "Now that you know where your power comes from, I'm sure she'll help you remember your true self. Like Nisa is always with me, Silaluk will be watching over you."

Ujurak turned his gaze to the sky. The stars had all faded into the early dawn light, but Kallik hoped he could feel the presence of the bear spirits, just the way she could.

"So it's settled, then," Toklo said, shifting impatiently. "You turn into a flat-face, walk into the pelt-den, and set Lusa free." He turned and began to lead the way toward the no-claw den at a fast trot. Kallik and Ujurak hurried to keep up with him.

"Um, just keep in mind that it might be more, uh—" Ujurak started to say.

"Let me guess," Toklo said, swinging his head around with a scornful look. "Complicated."

"Well, yes!" Ujurak said. "We don't know what's going on in there. It might be harder than it sounds. And besides, I want to free the other trapped animals, too."

"What?" Toklo roared. He skidded to a stop and spun around. "Are you out of your mind? There's no time for that!"

Ujurak stood his ground. "I will if I can," he said. "That's the deal. Otherwise I'm not changing shape at all."

Toklo pawed at the snow, growling deep in his throat.

"I think it's all right," Kallik tried to interject. "What harm could it do if he frees some seals and birds?"

"Fine," Toklo said. "As long as he understands that I might *eat* them while they're escaping."

Kallik let out a huff of amusement.

Ujurak poked Toklo with his nose. "Give me at least a day before you come charging in with your roaring and bossiness, okay?"

Toklo harrumphed. "Fine," he said. "But you'd better act as fast as you can. I'm still afraid Lusa will go into the longsleep while she's in there, if she hasn't already."

Kallik shivered again and sped up, feeling the sunbeams on her shoulders and smelling the heavy, sticky scent of oil in the air. As the three bears bounded across the snow, Kallik sent a quiet prayer to Nisa and the other bear spirits.

Please let this work. Please help us free Lusa. Please let her still be awake . . . and alive.

CHAPTER TWENTY-EIGHT

Ujurak

They stopped a few bearlengths from the pelt-den, near a flat area surrounded by tall chunks of ice. Ujurak could see flat-faces coming in and out of the pelt-den in a busy, urgent-looking way. Toklo nudged him and Kallik behind one of the large chunks of ice, out of sight of the flat-faces.

"Good luck," Kallik said, nosing Ujurak's side. "I know you can do it."

"We'll be ready to come in if you don't," Toklo added in his usual reassuring way.

Ujurak nodded. He was too anxious to talk. He was frightened that this would be the last time he looked down at thick brown paws—the last time he sniffed the wind with a brown bear's nose. But he had to be brave. He had to believe that his mother would be watching and protecting him.

He took a deep breath and thought about flat-faces. He knew he needed to look older than he had the last time. None of the flat-faces here were young cubs, and he didn't want to be sent away before he could do anything. He felt his body thinning and his fur shrinking back into his skin. Pale fingers appeared in place of his paws and bare toes replaced his paw-pads on the snow. He stopped being able to feel his hands and feet almost immediately. It was *freezing* out here. He'd forgotten about that part. If he didn't hurry, he'd freeze to death, but on the other hand, he couldn't exactly walk into the tent without a pelt on.

Rubbing his arms, Ujurak stared around, dancing on the snow to keep his feet out of it as much as possible. He barely noted the two bears watching him in astonishment. He spotted an empty snow vehicle not far away. Glancing over at the tent to make sure no one could see him, Ujurak darted over to the truck and jumped inside. To his relief, not only were the doors unlocked, but there were bundles of stuff in the back, including a few bags of clothes.

He pulled out a pair of thick gray wool trousers, a dark green work shirt, a warm black coat, thick brown socks, and a pair of solid brown boots. Everything was a little too big for him, which worried him. Was he old enough to fit in here?

Old enough to . . . what? He stopped for a moment, thinking. What was he doing? Why was he here? He glanced out the window of the vehicle and saw the large tent set up on the snow. He wasn't sure why, but he knew he needed to get in there. His gaze traveled on to the giant tower in the water. He knew it was an oil rig, and he could tell from the smell and the look of the water that there must have been an accident, and that oil had spilled into the sea.

Is that why I'm here? Something about the oil rig made his skin crawl. He instinctively wanted to get as far away from it as possible. That didn't seem like a normal human way to feel. He had a strange memory of oil clinging to him, coating his fur, but that didn't make any sense. For one thing, he didn't have fur.

Puzzled, Ujurak climbed out of the truck and headed toward the tent. He felt much warmer now; the clothes protected him comfortably from the freezing wind. Other people hurried by without really looking at him, dashing to their snowmobiles or carrying cages into the tent. He huddled into the coat, hoping none of them would recognize the clothes he had borrowed.

He hesitated for a moment outside the entrance, then pushed back the flap and ducked inside. A wave of warmth and animal smells hit him, and he stood for a moment, feeling overwhelmed. The tent was full of cages, from one wall to the other, all of them occupied by sick-looking seals or birds, the occasional walrus, and a bear or two. People in green jackets were bent over tables, cleaning oil from feathers and fur and murmuring to one another.

Something jolted inside him as he glanced at the nearest bear. It was huge and white, although streaked with oil stains through its matted fur. It looked old and feeble, and he felt a gnawing sense of pity that seemed to come from somewhere deep in his heart, as if he could identify with the sad old bear.

Because I can, he thought. *I've been a bear. And a seal. And a bird. I've been all of these animals.* His head felt muddled, but certain memories stood out clearly. The smell of the oil brought back some truly horrible ones.

Before he could look around any further, a tall man with dark skin and curly black hair strode up to him, frowning.

"Who are you?" the man asked, stepping between Ujurak and the cages. "I haven't seen you around before."

"I—uh—I'm, I'm Ujurak," Ujurak stammered. He thought quickly. "My dad works on the oil rig."

The strange man frowned even more. "Was he one of the ones out here yelling at us the other day? Telling us their job is more important than saving these animals here? Because if he sent you to convince us to let that other icebreaker ship through here, you can tell him it's not going to happen."

"Um," Ujurak said, confused. "No, he didn't—I mean, we feel bad about the spill. I just wanted to see if there was anything I could do to help." He glanced around at the oil-splattered wildlife. "It's all so horrible."

His voice broke, and the man's face softened. "Look, kid, we don't need any trouble."

"I won't be trouble!" Ujurak promised. "My dad won't mind that I'm here. Truly. There must be something I can do. I'm good with animals."

The tall man rubbed his chin for a moment, studying Ujurak. "All right," he said at last. "My name's Craig. I'm second in command of the international response team, here to help clean up after the oil spills." He snorted in a way that reminded Ujurak of someone. "It'd be a lot more useful if we could stop the spills *before* they happened, of course, but no one listens when you tell them that drilling up here isn't worth it." He flung out a hand toward a seabird lying miserably in a nearby cage.

"Nobody cares about the gulls and the seals and the polar bears. No matter how many pictures we take or how many reporters we call. By this point, they're like, 'Oh, another oil spill, boring. Call us when a celebrity gets drenched in oil, *then* maybe we'll be interested.'" Craig saw the baffled look on Ujurak's face and shook his head. "Sorry. This kind of thing gets me really worked up."

Ujurak couldn't believe it. Someone who felt the way he did about the oil! "It's not just birds and seals, either," he said. He had a vague memory of swimming through dark water that tasted like poison and an enormous beast nearly running him down as it churned through the water. "The beluga whales are really suffering, too. There's nothing for them to eat and the pollution in the water is making them sick."

Craig ran one hand through his hair. "Been doing your research, have you?" he said. "What else do you know about the whales?"

"Some of them have been killed by the—" Ujurak hunted for the right word. "Poisonbeast" popped into his head, but he had a feeling that wasn't the right thing to say here. "The large vehicles that swim," he finished lamely. "Underwater?"

"Submarines?" Craig asked. Ujurak nodded. That sounded right to him. Craig cracked a smile. "Fancy meeting a sixteen-year-old who doesn't know what a submarine is," he said. "Where've you been hiding, under a rock?"

Maybe, Ujurak thought. "This is not my first language," he explained. Technically that was true. He wasn't sure what he was supposed to be, but he knew he'd been something else before he was a human.

"Ah," Craig said, nodding. "Well, it doesn't surprise me that the submarines have killed some whales, although they always say they'll be real careful about their routes and everything." He shoved his hands in his coat pockets and rocked back and forth on his feet, looking troubled.

"It all seems so obvious to us," he said. "Of course when you disrupt the environment like this, the animals are going to suffer. When you fill the water with poison, everything dies. And we're all connected, so we shouldn't think we're safe just because we don't live in the Arctic. It starts with the gulls and the whales, but then—"

"Oh my gosh, Craig, did you really find someone who hasn't heard all your speeches yet?" A cheerful-looking girl bounced up behind Craig and grinned at Ujurak. "Escape while you can," she said with a wink. "He'll go on like this for days. Even here, where we obviously all agree with him."

Escape. Something about that word caught Ujurak's attention. That's what he was here for. Something about escaping.

Craig returned the girl's grin fondly. "I don't know what you have to be so cheerful about," he said. "It's your future we're mucking up."

"No, we're *fixing* it," she said, whapping him on the arm. "Look at all these animals we're helping! We're making a difference!"

Craig rolled his eyes. "Ujurak, this is Sally. Our perpetual optimist."

Sally held out her hand and Ujurak shook it tentatively. She had shoulder-length dark hair and laughing dark eyes, and she looked about the same age that Ujurak was in this form. Her smile was wide and friendly, and she laughed easily. She reminded him very strongly of someone—someone close to him—but he couldn't think who. He couldn't remember anyone he knew at all.

"Why don't I show you around?" Sally suggested. "Save you from Craig's sermons, give you something to do?"

"Okay," Ujurak said.

Craig laughed. "Guess I can't compete with that. Just be careful, you two. These are still wild animals, however helpless they might seem right now." He clapped Ujurak on the shoulder. "And thanks for coming. We appreciate all the help we can get." Craig lifted the flap and ducked out of the tent. Ujurak heard him calling to someone outside.

"So you probably saw the smaller tents outside." Sally started talking as soon as Craig was gone. "That's where we sleep, or at least, take turns sleeping—we've been so busy in here, we can't take much of a break. All these animals need to be cleaned and fed and tranquilized again, plus of course we're still figuring out where to take all of them once they're healthy enough to be released back into the wild."

"You're going to release them into the wild?" Ujurak asked, surprised. He wasn't sure why, but he'd thought the humans were going to keep the animals locked up forever.

216 SEEKERS: FIRE IN THE SKY

Sally gave him a funny look. "Of course. What else would we do with a bunch of seagulls and walruses?"

"Um," Ujurak said. "I don't know."

She took his arm and tugged him forward, pointing to a seal in one of the cages. It looked up at them with large, limpid black eyes. Oil clung to its gray flippers and long whiskers. "Look at that poor thing," she said. "She was just swimming along, minding her own business, when a bunch of oil got dumped on top of her. You should have seen her when they brought her in! She was slick with oil from head to tail. It's amazing she could breathe at all. She wouldn't have survived if we hadn't put her straight into some warm water and cleaned her off. We still have some work to do, but she's looking much better now."

Sally crouched and pulled a silver bowl out of the bottom of the seal's cage. "Want to feed her?" she offered. "It's easy."

"Sure," Ujurak said, feeling a little more confident. Sally acted as if it was absolutely natural for him to be here, and it made him feel as though he could actually help. She showed him where they kept a cooler of dead fish on ice for the seals. He took one between his fingers and dropped it through the bars of the cage into the seal's mouth. She swallowed it and made a low barking noise.

"Aw, she said, 'Thank you!'" Sally said, beaming.

"Actually, I'm pretty sure she said, 'Another! At once!'" Ujurak explained.

Sally started laughing. "That's hilarious!"

Ujurak took another fish and fed it to the seal, trying to hide his expression. He wasn't used to being called funny—especially when he hadn't meant to be. He'd actually understood the seal's language, and that's what she had said.

"Oh, let me show you the weirdest one we found!" Sally said, pulling his elbow to steer him around. She guided him past the large polar bear and pointed to a smaller cage a few feet away, closer to the center of the tent. "Check it out. That's a *black* bear!"

Ujurak looked at the small black cub curled up inside the cage, and his heart nearly stopped. He *knew* her.

It was Lusa!

That was who Sally reminded him of, he realized. She had the same bright, happy spirit as Lusa. His memories came flooding back. He was a bear—a brown bear. He was here to free Lusa. Toklo and Kallik were waiting outside. That's what he was here for. And his mother was somewhere above, watching over him. *Hang on to that*, he reminded himself.

He remembered the last time he was a flat-face, and how much smaller he had been. He felt more confident now, more comfortable inside his human skin. He wondered if that was because he was in the shape of an older flat-face this time, or if it was because he could remember some of the things he'd learned before.

Lusa stared at him through the bars, her eyes bright and startled. He wondered if she recognized him. He stepped toward her, thinking he should say something to her in bear language and let her know who he was and that she was safe now.

"Hey!" Sally said. She caught his sleeve and yanked him back. "Don't get too close! You heard what Craig said. She's a wild bear. I mean, I know she's wicked cute, but she could still be dangerous."

So could I, Ujurak thought. *I'm a wild bear, too.*

"Sorry," he said.

"That's okay," Sally said, smiling again. "I'm a little bit in love with her myself. Isn't she the cutest? We totally thought she was a polar bear when she came in all covered in oil. That's until we started scrubbing, and her fur stayed black! We have *no idea* what a black bear is doing out here on the ice. I mean, it doesn't make any sense at all. The poor baby must be so hungry and confused."

"Can I feed her, too?" Ujurak asked.

To his disappointment, Sally shook her head. "No, only Tara and Erica are allowed to handle or feed her. They know what they're doing. We can work with the animals that are less likely to claw our faces off."

Indignant, Ujurak nearly said, "Lusa wouldn't do that!" But he caught himself just in time, and nodded instead. "Okay." He'd have to find another way to get close to her.

He remembered the other part of his mission—to release the rest of the birds and seals and animals in here. Except now he knew that they would be free eventually. Sally had said they'd all be going back to the wild, and in the meanwhile the humans were taking care of them. So they didn't need his help. All he had to do was save Lusa.

"Besides, Tara fed her recently," Sally went on. "She's

practically gone through our entire stock of canned fruit already! But we'll be getting more supplies tomorrow when our ship arrives."

Suddenly there was a commotion at the entrance of the tent. A dark-haired woman pushed her way in and called, "Quick, clear the tables! We have another batch coming in!"

All the people in the tent sprang into action, putting animals back into cages and wiping down the tables. More people in green coats came in the front carrying nets and cages. Ujurak's heart lurched as he saw the sad state of the birds and animals inside. Oil dripped from their feathers, and most of them were entirely motionless. He couldn't believe any of them were alive with that much poison saturating their skin.

"Come on!" Sally said. "This is where you can really help!" She dragged him over to the nearest table and handed him a pair of gloves. Ujurak pulled them on as Sally introduced him to Erica, the dark-haired woman who'd led the way in. She gently extracted a long-necked bird from one of the nets and laid it out on the table. Ujurak saw her pull a tiny dart out of its side.

"It's tranquilized," Sally pointed out, seeing the direction of his gaze. "That way it won't wake up and panic in the middle of this."

Ujurak was relieved to hear that it wasn't dead. He followed Erica's instructions as she showed him how to remove the oil from its feathers and gently wipe off the beak, eyes, and webbed feet with a soft, bubbly mixture.

Erica moved on to the next table, and Ujurak and Sally

worked for a while in silence. Every time he looked up, Sally grinned at him.

"Isn't this great?" she whispered. "We're totally helping! I'm so lucky my parents let me come up here and do this."

Ujurak had to admit, it made him feel better, too. He could see the difference immediately in the bird's feathers. His nimble flat-face hands worked quickly and efficiently, and he felt connected to the other people around him, all of whom were working hard on the same thing. He couldn't believe there were this many flat-faces willing to spend their time just helping and saving animals.

True, the damage was from something the flat-faces themselves had done to them. But maybe Lusa was right after all. Maybe the flat-faces weren't all bad, and maybe some of them could make a difference. If he hadn't had his friends and his life as a bear to go back to, he could imagine staying in this form and doing work like this for the rest of his life.

He glanced over at Lusa's cage. She had her eyes fixed on him and her head was tilted curiously. He smiled at her, and she blinked.

Don't worry, Lusa, he promised silently. *I won't forget this time. I know who I am and why I'm here. And I'll get you out of here. I promise.*

CHAPTER TWENTY-NINE

Lusa

It was Ujurak. Lusa was sure now. The way the flat-face boy looked at her and smiled—it gave her the same warm, secure feeling that being with Ujurak did.

When he first walked in, she'd wondered why he looked familiar. For a while she'd watched him, thinking that perhaps she'd seen him around the Bear Bowl. He didn't look the way Ujurak had looked the last time he became a flat-face. This time he was bigger and his hair was a bit lighter, and he moved with an odd new confidence, as if he felt more comfortable being a flat-face than he had before. Even his flat-face chatter sounded deeper and wiser, as if he knew more words and flat-face ideas than he had before.

But there was something about his scent that still smelled a bit like Ujurak. It had to be him. He'd come to rescue her! She hoped that meant that Kallik was here, too, waiting just outside the pelt walls somewhere. Lusa loved the idea of the four of them being together again. *I hope they found Toklo. I hope he's all right.*

She peered up through the bars at the table where Ujurak was working next to the dark-haired girl. They were talking and laughing as if they'd known each other for ages. Lusa had seen them start with a bird, but now they were cleaning off a droopy-looking seal. She wondered if Ujurak's stomach growled when he saw it. She wasn't at all interested in eating it, but she was sure Toklo and Kallik would be!

Ujurak's delicate new paws worked gently on the seal's fur, rubbing something bubbly onto it and then carefully cleaning out the oil. He looked as kind and capable as the flat-faces who had worked on her when she came in. He also looked as if he was having a good time. Lusa couldn't remember him looking so happy, certainly not since they'd been out on the ice. He'd been worrying so much about the oil and the flat-faces, he'd barely said a word the last couple of days they'd been together.

Now he was chattering away in a funny flat-face voice. Lusa wished she could understand what he was saying. What was his plan for rescuing her? How would he get her out past all the other flat-faces? She settled back on her hindquarters. She wasn't worried. Ujurak would figure it out; he always did.

The same dark-haired female as before came back with another bowl of fruit. Lusa licked it up gratefully. She loved the tingle of sweetness on her tongue and the taste of the juice sliding down her throat.

"That's not bear food," grunted a voice nearby.

Lusa jumped and looked around. The old white bear was

awake, squinting at her through the bars of his cage. He looked disoriented and unhappy. Even though he'd been washed by the flat-faces, his fur was still a sickly gray color.

"It is for black bears," she told him.

"Huh," he said, sniffing at a bowl of meat sitting in his cage. "And you trust them enough to eat it? If it comes from the no-claws, it's probably poisonous."

"No, no," Lusa said. "It's good, I promise. You should eat if you're hungry."

"Huh," he said again. He gave the bowl a doubtful glance, but Lusa could see that he was tempted. "What is going on in here? Why do they have us trapped like this?" He stood up and turned in an awkward circle inside his cage. One of his large paws swatted at the bars. "When I get my claws on them, I'll show them how a white bear should be treated!"

"Wait, don't get excited," Lusa said, trying to sound soothing. "The flat-faces are just trying to help, I promise."

He squinted at her again. "What's a flat-face?"

"Um," Lusa said. "Oh. I mean the no-claws. We call them flat-faces."

"Huh," he grunted.

"But these are the good kind of, uh, no-claws," Lusa said. "They're taking care of us and feeding us and trying to clean us up."

"Clean us up!" the old bear snorted. He glared at one of his gray, sticky paws. "They're the ones who created this mess in the first place!"

"I know," Lusa said. "But I think that was a different group of flat-faces. Some of them are bad and some of them are good. Kind of like bears."

"No bear is as bad as a no-claw," he growled.

Lusa thought about Shoteka, the giant grizzly who had gone after Toklo even though Toklo was just a cub. But at least Shoteka never had a firestick. "That's probably true," she allowed. "Yet some flat-faces are actually very kind. I grew up in a place where flat-faces fed us and healed us if we got sick."

The old bear looked shocked. "There's no such place!"

"There is!" Lusa insisted. "It's called the Bear Bowl. My mother and father and friends are still there. Flat-faces come to visit every day, and some of them bring food and even play with us."

"Sounds unnatural," the white bear grumbled. He sighed heavily and looked down at his paws. "But I guess I wouldn't have gotten clean without them. I never thought I'd see the day when I'd need help from a no-claw."

"There's nothing wrong with accepting help when you need it," Lusa said.

"White bears can take care of themselves!" he snapped. "That's how it was when I was a cub, anyway. We had sky-lengths of endless ice to walk without ever seeing a no-claw or firebeast. Seals practically threw themselves out of the sea for us to eat. I remember my mother telling us stories of Silaluk and teaching us to fight." He shook his head. "She was killed by a firebeast. That was the first time I ever saw one. And they've just kept coming, more and more of them all the time. Now the ice is full of no-claws and their burning, choking smells and their horrible smoke."

Lusa felt terribly sad for the old bear. His head drooped and his paws trembled with exhaustion and fear.

"I don't know what's going to happen to me," he sighed finally.

"Maybe you can come with us," Lusa offered. "My friends are going to rescue me soon. I can tell them to free you at the same time, and we'll go out on the ice together. It's easier with friends. Less lonely, and less scary."

The white bear shook his head. "I don't have the energy for it anymore," he told her. "Everything has changed so much. It's all so hard." He sighed again. "Perhaps the no-claws can look after me better than I can look after myself right now."

Lusa wished she could lean into his fur and make him feel better. She wanted to tell him that she was going to save the wild with Ujurak and the others, but she was afraid it would sound ridiculous. The way he described the changes . . . how could four little bears do anything about that?

"No," the white bear said, staring at the flat-faces bustling around the pelt-den. "It's no use." He lay down, rested his chin on his paws, and closed his eyes. "The world I knew is gone," he said sadly. "And it's never coming back."

CHAPTER THIRTY

Toklo

The sun was slowly sinking below the edge of the sky. Ujurak had been inside the pelt-den the entire day, and it was driving Toklo wild with anxiety. There'd been no sign of him or Lusa. Toklo hated not knowing what was going on. He stood up and shook out his fur, scattering small wet drops of snow around him.

"Toklo, just keep still," Kallik complained. "I've told you, creeping up to the pelt-den over and over again is only going to get you caught. All your pacing hasn't told you anything yet, has it?"

"I might smell something new this time," Toklo growled. "I'll be right back." He crept out from behind the chunk of ice where they'd been hiding for most of the day. They'd seen flat-faces charging in and out of the pelt-den. At one point a whole crowd of them had arrived on several firebeasts and carried a line of oil-soaked animals into the den. It had been very noisy, and the commotion inside the pelt-den afterward went on for a long time. And it still didn't give Toklo any clues about what was happening.

Toklo was baffled. What did the flat-faces want with the sick animals? Did they love their oil so much that they had to save it any way they could—even if it meant squeezing it out of feathers and fur? He wanted to know what would happen to the animals afterward. From the scent of the pelt-den, most of them were still alive in there. Including Lusa . . . he kept catching her scent mingled with all the others.

He realized that Kallik was crawling along close behind him. They were only a few bearlengths from the back wall of the pelt-den at this point. The dark green wall rippled in front of them, and the high-pitched chatter of flat-face voices leaked out. Was one of them Ujurak's?

"We should have told Ujurak to send us a sign," he growled to Kallik. "Now we don't even know if he remembers that he's a bear—or why he's in there."

"He told us to give him some time," Kallik said. "I'm sure he remembers. He'll do what he promised." She glanced at the slumbering firebeasts. "Toklo, we're way too close. Can we please go back to our hiding spot?"

"Shhhh," he said fiercely. "I'm listening." He padded a few steps closer and strained his ears toward the pelt-den.

"Oh," Kallik said in a sarcastic voice. "Wonderful. Because *that* will help."

He growled at her and took another step toward the den. Of course, she was right. He didn't want to admit it, but nothing he heard from the den told him anything. He took a deep breath in, but the smells were equally mysterious. There was no way to know what was happening inside unless he clawed open the walls himself.

He was sorely tempted to do just that. Frustrated, he pawed at the snow.

"You know what would be really unhelpful?" Kallik said. "If we got captured by flat-faces, too. That would be spectacularly useless."

"We're not going to—" Toklo snapped, whirling on her. But his words were interrupted by a huge roar. Toklo nearly leaped out of his skin as a firebeast only slightly bigger than him came tearing around the side of the pelt-den. Its eyes blazed and its roaring was louder than most full-grown bears. It raced at him and Kallik as if it was preparing to attack.

"Run!" Kallik shouted. She bundled into Toklo, shoving him aside as the firebeast whooshed past. They both scrambled around and bolted for the safety of the ice field. The roaring slowed behind them and then stopped. By the time Toklo and Kallik were crouched, panting, behind their chunk of ice again, the firebeast was resting outside the entrance of the pelt-den.

"It wasn't chasing us at all," Toklo grumbled.

"Yes, but that doesn't mean it wouldn't have hit us!" Kallik said. "Especially since we were right in its way! *Now* will you settle down, please?"

Toklo bristled angrily. His frustration came boiling up from deep inside, and he bared his teeth at her. "Stop telling me what to do!" he snarled.

"Stop acting like a stupid squirrel, then!" Kallik snarled

back. He realized how much bigger she'd grown than him. But he was still sure he could fight her, and this time Ujurak and Lusa weren't there to stop them.

They were standing nose to nose, and he had his paw lifted to strike at her throat, when he saw the look on her face shift from hostile to concerned. She turned to look at the pelt-den, sniffing the air.

"What?" he asked, lowering his paw. "Do you smell something?"

"I thought I did," she said. "I think I can tell which no-claw scent is Ujurak's. But it's all muddled up with the other smells in there. I wish my nose were more helpful!" She clawed at her muzzle, and he realized that she was just as worried and terrified as he was. They didn't need to take their fear out on each other's pelts.

Toklo took a step back and grunted with exasperation. "This is horrible," he said.

"I know," Kallik agreed with a sigh. She lay down and buried her nose in the snow for a moment. "I wish there was something we could do."

"I'm the one who was supposed to look after them," Toklo said, scraping at the block of ice. "Both of them, Ujurak and Lusa. I always take care of them. But now they're both in danger, and here I am just hanging around like a useless lump of fur." He remembered the star-bear's words about one of them dying. What if Ujurak or Lusa was on the edge of death right that moment, and he was just sitting outside watching the pelt-den instead of trying to save them?

"I know how you feel," Kallik said. "Really I do. But remember, they're not exactly helpless, either of them. Lusa understands flat-faces . . . she knows all about them and she's not even that scared of them. She's probably doing better in there than you or I would. And Ujurak *is* a flat-face right now. With his powers, and guided by the spirits the way he is, he'll know what to do. I'm sure they'll be all right."

Toklo grunted and lay down next to her. "We'll see."

"You know what we should do?" Kallik said, sitting up in a rush and spraying snow all over him. "We should hunt. We need to keep our strength up anyway, in case we have to make a speedy escape tonight. That's probably the best way we can help." She nudged his side. "Besides, it'll keep us from worrying so much. Come on."

Toklo wanted to stay and watch the pelt-den, but as soon as Kallik had said the word "hunt," he felt the enormous, gnawing ache in his stomach. He couldn't remember the last time he'd eaten. Was it back on the floating firebeast with Lusa?

"All right," he said grudgingly, climbing to his paws.

"This might take me a moment," Kallik said, turning her nose into the wind. "There are so many seal smells coming from the pelt-den . . . I have to separate out the ones coming from farther away. . . . Let me think." She closed her eyes and inhaled deeply, slowly twisting her head one way and then the other.

"There!" she said. Her eyes popped open. "Let's go!" She sprang to her paws and started to run across the ice.

Toklo followed her, impressed. How could she smell

something so far away? He knew his nose was excellent, but it was so clogged with the oil scent that he doubted he'd be able to find a seal hole even if it was under his paws right now.

They ran and ran, sprinting up snowy hills and tumbling down the other side, skidding on slippery patches and jumping over small cracks in the ice. Sometimes Kallik would stop to sniff the air and peer at the bubbles underneath her. Toklo had to admit he loved the feeling of the wind in his fur. He already felt better, just from stretching his legs and getting a chance to run. It was much more satisfying than crouching in the snow and staring at flat-faces all day long.

Finally Kallik slid to a stop and pointed with her nose. Toklo saw the dark hole in the ice up ahead. It looked very still, and he couldn't smell any recent scents of seal. But he watched Kallik slowly creep up and lay down next to the hole. Then he copied her movements, trying to be just as quiet and stealthy. He imagined he was stalking a rabbit through the forest, placing his paws carefully among the leaves and branches. Here it was ice and snow, but the cautious pawsteps were the same.

Kallik fixed her eyes on the hole. Her breathing slowed down until Toklo could barely see her fur rising and falling. She seemed to have forgotten that he was there. He stared at the dark water, too. It was still hard for him to wait patiently for prey to come to him. He wanted to rush at the water and attack moving shapes with his claws, the way he caught salmon. But he already knew that that wouldn't work out here.

His ears pricked forward as something rippled below the surface. His eyes flicked to Kallik and he saw that she had turned her eyes to him as well. With a tiny movement of her head, she motioned from him to the hole.

"You should get it," he whispered back.

"Just try," she said softly. "I know you can do it."

He was about to argue with her, when a sleek brown head popped out of the water. Immediately his instincts took over and he lunged forward. For a moment his claws sliced through air, and he was afraid that he'd missed it. But then they sank into rubbery flesh, and he yanked the seal toward him, burying his teeth in its neck. Shaking it ferociously, he dragged it back up onto the ice and pinned it down until the thrashing stopped.

"You did it!" Kallik crowed. "That was perfect!"

Toklo wiped blood off his muzzle and licked his paws. "I did, didn't I?" he said smugly. "That wasn't so hard."

Kallik looked offended. Quickly Toklo ducked his head and muttered, "Well, perhaps it was a little hard."

The white bear bumped his side in a friendly way and crouched beside the seal. They tore long strips of flesh off and chewed, watching the sun disappear and the dark shadows creep across the ice. Toklo glanced up at the stars. It was easier to feel confident about saving Lusa when his belly was full. Maybe the others were even right about bear spirits watching over them.

They polished off the seal in no time, and then Toklo stood up, rubbing his paws into the snow. "We'd better get back," he said. "We should be there when whatever Ujurak is going to do happens." The anxiety was returning, prickling through his pelt.

"Absolutely," Kallik said, getting to her paws as well. "Race you there!" She sprinted off across the snow.

"Hey!" he shouted. "No fair! Your paws are better on the ice, and you know where we're going, and you got a head start—" He realized she wasn't slowing down, so he stopped complaining and started to run. The cold night wind chilled his nose and made his eyes water. But his paws felt strong and powerful, and he flew across the snow as fast as any white bear. He kept Kallik in his sights as he ran.

Toklo cast a glance up at the stars. He *hoped* the others were right about the bear spirits, and that the star-bear who had told him one of them would die was wrong. If there was any night when they could use serious spirit help, this was it.

CHAPTER THIRTY-ONE

Ujurak

Ujurak peeled off his gloves and dunked his pale human hands into a bucket of warm water. He felt exhausted, but in a happy, useful sort of way. He'd spent the whole day helping Sally, and he hadn't had to spend a moment of it trying to figure out what the right thing to do was. He was surprised to realize how much he liked not being in charge. It was much easier when someone just told you what to do, and when you knew that everything you were doing was making the world a better place, even in a small way.

He'd never thought that being a flat-face could be so satisfying.

Sally came up beside him and dipped her hands into the water as well. Their fingers brushed, and he looked up to see her smiling at him.

"I guess you have to go back to your dad now," she said ruefully.

"My dad?" Ujurak said, then caught himself. "Oh, yeah, of course. On the oil rig. Yeah. But just for the night. I'll come back tomorrow." He glanced around at the room of animals. Many of them were sleeping, exhausted by the stressful day or carefully tranquilized so they could rest. Lusa was one of the few still awake. She tilted her head at him when he looked at her.

He wished he could tell her he wasn't really leaving. He'd pretend to go, and then he'd sneak back in and let her out in the middle of the night.

Unless... Ujurak wondered if it would be so bad if he spent one more day as a human, especially since he didn't seem to be in danger of forgetting his bear-ness right now. There was still so much work to do with the animals. He could really be a help to Sally and Craig and the others. And Lusa was warm and safe and well fed here. It wouldn't hurt her to spend another day in the tent.

But he'd have to let Toklo and Kallik know so they wouldn't come tearing in here themselves.

He was scrubbing at his hands, thinking about how to get a message to them, when Sally said, "I'm glad you're coming back tomorrow. It'll be pretty crazy again because our ship is coming, so we'll be unloading supplies and then loading it with all the animals going back to the mainland."

Ujurak's stomach lurched. "Going back to the mainland?" he echoed.

"Yeah," Sally said. "The ones in the best shape—we'll get them as far away from here as possible." She nodded over at Lusa. "That includes our cute little friend there. They'll take her back to a forest where she belongs. I bet you'll be happy about that, won't you, sweetheart?" she said to Lusa in a friendly voice. "Gosh, poor little thing. She's probably ready to hibernate about now."

"Yeah, she is," Ujurak said. He barely noticed the strange look Sally gave him. His head was swirling with guilt and worry and confusion. All the fears he'd managed to push back while he was working during the day flooded through him again.

Tonight was his last chance to rescue Lusa. But was it the right thing to do? The kind humans were ready to take her back to the land, where she would be safe. Was that what Lusa really wanted? Would she resent him for keeping her on the ice instead?

Then he remembered the signs in the sky—the cloud trail and the tiny stars. All four of them had to finish the journey. Surely Lusa knew that, too. If he could only talk to her, then he could make sure she was willing to come with him. But there was no chance of that happening with Sally watching him all the time.

He looked up and realized that Sally was giving him a puzzled look. "Are you all right?" she asked. "It looked like you kind of drifted off into space for a minute there."

"Sorry," he said, although he didn't exactly understand what she'd said. "I'd better get going."

"Yeah, sure," she said. To his surprise, she took one of his hands and squeezed it. "Thanks for your help today. You're a natural at this. It's like you could understand what the animals were feeling."

Ujurak shifted uncomfortably. "I was just guessing," he mumbled.

"Well, you should think about doing this forever," Sally said, grinning. "We could roam the world, saving animals wherever we go. Like wildlife superheroes. Wouldn't that be awesome?"

He looked down at her hand, still twined through his. "Yeah, it would be," he said. "But—I can't."

"Oh." Sally looked hurt for a moment. She let go of his hand and pushed her hair back behind her ears, avoiding his eyes. "Okay. I mean . . . you mean because of your dad? He wouldn't let you?"

"Sort of." Ujurak felt bad lying to her, but what else could he say? *"Sorry, I'm actually a bear"?* He could just imagine the look on her face if he said that.

"Well, he can't control you forever," Sally said, tossing her head.

"It's not just that," Ujurak said. "I have these . . . friends . . . they need me. We're—it's kind of a responsibility, uh, thing. It's hard to explain."

"Ah," Sally said with a smile. "It's complicated, huh? I've heard that before."

Ujurak nearly laughed. He wondered what Toklo would say about this conversation. "Yeah," he said. "Complicated."

"Sure, okay," Sally said. She looked away again. "Maybe you can tell me about it tomorrow."

I'll be gone tomorrow, he thought. He gazed into her dark, laughing eyes and wished he could tell her the truth.

"Well, good night," she said. She headed toward the front flap and he followed her. Outside, they stopped and looked at each other awkwardly for a moment.

"I'm going this way," she said finally, crooking her thumb at the sleeping tent and smiling.

"Right," he said. "And me this way." He pointed out at the oil rig.

"See you tomorrow." She waved and turned away.

"Bye." He watched her disappear into the sleeping tent. He wanted to run straight to Toklo and Kallik, but Craig was nearby, talking to someone in a firebeast, and Erica was outside the main tent, gathering snow in a bucket. He waved to both of them and started walking toward the oil rig.

It was much colder now that night had fallen. A pale moon glowed overhead, lighting his path toward the gloomy tower out on the water. Ujurak glanced back several times until he saw that Craig and Erica had gone inside again. Not many people were still out and about. He figured he was far enough away that no one would notice him doubling back.

He trotted in a wide circle around the tents, keeping an eye out for any people. He saw no signs of Toklo or Kallik either; hopefully they were waiting for him well out of sight.

Ujurak snuck behind the tents and found a pair of big snow vehicles parked and empty. Both were unlocked. Carefully, he opened the first door and crawled inside. He rummaged through the stuff in the back, looking for tools that would help him free Lusa. Even if she decided not to come with him, he at least had to give her the choice to be saved.

He found a long black stick, and when he pressed a button on the side, light poured out one end. Startled, Ujurak dropped it and had to search for it under the seat.

Flashlight, he thought as he hefted it in his hands again. It was strange how he somehow knew the right word for it, and yet he'd been surprised by what it did. He hit the button one more time and the light went out. This could be useful, especially with the feeble human eyes he had to work with.

He also found a pair of enormous clipperlike things with sharp edges. He turned them over, gently touching the blades to see how sharp they were. He was pretty sure Lusa's cage had a lock on it that needed a key. But perhaps he could break it using something like this instead. He lifted the clippers and realized how heavy they were. He'd have to move carefully while he was carrying them.

After that he waited, hiding inside the firebeast, until he was sure that everyone would be asleep. The moon was high in the sky, which was packed with glittering stars. His weak human body shivered as he climbed out into the freezing cold again. He couldn't wait to have all his fur back.

Snow crunched under his boots, no matter how lightly he tried to walk. But there was no sound from the sleeping tent, and all the lamps were off inside the main tent. Ujurak crept around to the front and ducked through the flap.

A few of the animals stirred sleepily. It was very dark inside the tent, and Ujurak wished he had his bear's eyes. He pulled out the flashlight he'd found inside the snow vehicle. He pointed it at the floor and hit the button, shading the light with his other hand.

The tiny warm beam guided him between the cages and tables until he found Lusa's cage. She woke up as he moved toward her and blinked blindly into the light.

"Sorry," Ujurak whispered, turning the light back down to the floor. "Lusa, it's me. It's Ujurak. You know me, right?" He remembered communicating with his bear friends in their own language the last time he was a human. But the growls and rumbles he needed felt buried farther down in his mind than before, and he didn't have time to dredge them back up. He felt sure that Lusa would understand him even if he didn't speak bear to her right now.

Lusa hooked her claws in the side of the cage and gazed back at him with bright eyes. He reached through the bars and stroked her soft head. She nudged at his hand with her nose, then licked his fingers.

"I'm getting you out of here," he promised, scratching behind her ear. He crouched and studied the lock on her cage. As he'd expected, it required a key—he'd seen a ring of keys on Craig's belt earlier, so he guessed that those opened most of the cages. But he hoped he could snap the lock off with the clippers.

"Stand back," he said to Lusa, waving his hands at her. She tilted her head again, then slowly took a few steps back until she was pressed against the far wall of the cage.

Ujurak braced the clippers around the curved silver hoop of the lock. He leaned into the handles with all the force he could muster. *Boy, a bear's strength would be really useful right now!*

A long anxious moment passed as he grunted and strained. Suddenly there was a loud *SNAP!* and the lock broke in two. The heavy pieces went clattering to the floor with a noise that sounded deafening to Ujurak.

"Quick!" he whispered, swinging the door open. "Lusa, hurry!"

The little black cub darted out of the cage and gave him a grateful look. He started to lead the way out of the tent, then realized she had turned toward another cage.

"What is it?" he whispered, hurrying back to her. She had her nose pressed to the bars. Inside, the old male polar bear was sound asleep.

Ujurak was torn. If Lusa wanted him to rescue the old bear, he had to do it—but he was afraid that someone might have heard the noise of Lusa's lock breaking. What if flat-faces were heading for the tent right now? He didn't want to risk having to fight them off.

Then Lusa sighed a little and turned away from the bear's cage. She bumped Ujurak's leg with her nose and padded away toward the entrance.

Confused but relieved, Ujurak followed her. As they got to the door, he switched off the flashlight. Outside, the moon would be enough light for them, especially once he turned back into a bear.

Ujurak slipped out of the tent first. He turned to hold the flap open for Lusa and then jumped as someone shone a flashlight into his face.

"I knew it!" said Sally's voice. Ujurak lifted his hands to try to block the light from his eyes. "I knew I saw you sneaking around. What are you *doing?*"

"I, uh—" Ujurak started. Then Lusa nosed her way out of the tent and nearly crashed into him.

Sally gasped and the light fell away from his face. "That's the black bear!" she cried. "It got loose!"

"Actually, I freed her," Ujurak admitted. He could sense Lusa's nervousness in the way she was shuffling her paws and making small noises deep in her throat. He reached down and rested his hand reassuringly on her head.

In the moonlight, he saw Sally's mouth drop open. "You're crazy," she said, taking a step back. "You can't just—but she's—how—"

"Sally, this is Lusa," Ujurak said. "She's one of the friends I mentioned before."

Sally looked too thunderstruck to speak.

Ujurak was about to go on, when suddenly a light came on in the sleeping tent. He heard voices calling to one another and clattering that he was sure came from those sticks that made animals go to sleep.

"I'm sorry I can't explain," he said to Sally. "We have to go. Lusa, run!"

He shoved Lusa toward the ice field where he hoped Toklo and Kallik were still waiting. She pelted past Sally and scrambled up the slope. Her small black body stood out against the snowy backdrop, lit up by the silver moon.

Ujurak threw off his coat and shirt as he felt his body changing. His arms grew thicker and brown fur sprouted from his skin. His hands reached toward the ground, shifting into massive paws with thorn-sharp claws on the end. He shook off the work boots and pants as the last changes rippled through him. He was a bear once more.

Sally had her hands pressed to her face. He dipped his head to her, feeling waves of regret washing through him, and then bolted after Lusa. Behind him, the voices turned into shouts, and he heard flat-faces running across the snow toward Sally.

He dug his paws into the snow and ran faster. Above him, he could feel the warm glow of his mother's constellation gazing down at him. This was his path, and he would follow it where it led . . . now and forever.

CHAPTER THIRTY-TWO

Kallik

Kallik bounded to her paws when she heard the commotion down by the pelt-den.

"Something's happening!" she barked.

Toklo was already standing at the top of the slope, staring at the pelt-den. "I can't tell what's going on," he said. "It's too dark. There are shapes outside, but they could just be more flat-faces—or—" Suddenly he gasped. "I think I can see Lusa!"

Kallik pressed up next to him. Her heart was pounding. Were Lusa and Ujurak all right? All she could see outside the pelt-den was a couple of shadowy figures that looked like flat-faces. Then she spotted a small blur of shadows next to one of them. That could be Lusa!

"We should get down there," Toklo growled, taking a step forward. "They need our help!"

"Wait!" Kallik yelped. She shoved herself in his way. "Look!" The small blur separated from the other shadows and began running toward them. Kallik could tell right away from its funny rolling gait that it was Lusa. She was free!

"Where's Ujurak?" Toklo muttered fretfully. "Why isn't he right behind her?"

Then they saw one of the flat-faces start to change. His shadow grew bigger and bigger, and a moment later, a brown bear was dashing across the snow toward them, right on Lusa's paws.

"Over here!" Kallik shouted, leaping up on her hind legs and waving her paws. "We're here! Lusa! Ujurak!"

The two bears veered toward her, galloping up the incline. Kallik wanted to roar with joy when she saw Lusa's face only a bearlength away. The black bear cub threw herself at Kallik, knocking her over into the snow, and they rolled happily for a moment.

"I thought I'd never see you again!" Lusa cried.

"Same to you!" Kallik said. "What are you doing, letting yourself get caught by no-claws?"

"But they were nice," Lusa protested. "They cleaned me up. See?" She spun in a circle, showing off her shining coat.

Toklo snorted. "Only you would enjoy being caught by flat-faces."

"You're just jealous," Lusa teased, "because your pelt is still sticky and smelly. Maybe you should go down there and ask them to give you a bath, too."

"Not on your life!" Toklo growled. "No flat-face is putting its paws all over me!"

Lusa bumped against him. "Well, I guess you don't smell *that* bad."

He harrumphed and muttered grumpily. Lusa gave Kallik a twinkling glance, and Kallik sighed with relief. She hadn't seen Lusa this awake since they'd been out on the ice. It was nice to have their cheerful little friend back to herself again. Kallik hoped it could last—she knew the longsleep was still waiting to take Lusa, and they were heading back into a world of hard journeys and food that disagreed with the black bear.

Toklo sniffed Ujurak as he caught up. "You smell like flat-faces," he said disapprovingly.

"It's nice to see you, too," Ujurak joked.

"We'd better run," Toklo said. "Those flat-faces will be after you any moment now."

Ujurak shook his head. "Sally will stop them. I mean, she was pretty shocked, but—I think she understood."

"*Sally?*" Toklo grumbled. "What kind of name is that?"

"Lusa," Ujurak said urgently. "You can still go back if you want to."

Kallik stared at him. What was he talking about? Freeing Lusa was the whole point!

"Why would I do that?" Lusa asked, equally puzzled.

"They were planning to take you back to the mainland tomorrow," Ujurak said. "I know . . . I mean, I know that's what you wanted . . . before. If that's still what you want—" He paused, looking despairing, then burst out, "But we need you, Lusa! We need you to come with us. I saw more signs—we can't do this without you. All four of us have to be—"

Lusa pressed her nose into his thick fur and he stopped. "It's all right," she said. "You're right. We're going together."

She gave Toklo a significant look. "No matter what happens. This is our destiny."

Kallik glanced at Toklo, expecting him to argue. But the big brown bear just ducked his head and glared at the ice under his paws. Ujurak looked at him, too, and then let out his breath in a long sigh.

"Thank you," he murmured. "It won't be long now. I can feel it. Our journey will be over soon, I promise."

"Well, let's get a move on, then," Toklo growled, glancing at the pelt-den below them. More lights had come on and flat-faces were milling about outside, but it looked as if Ujurak was right. None of them had come after the bears.

Kallik took the lead as the bears turned their back on the flat-faces and began to run. She could feel her friends' fur brushing against her on either side—white and black and brown together. And as they ran, Kallik felt another bear running with them, huge and weightless, her paws skimming the ice. She turned and saw how Ujurak's eyes were shining, and she knew he felt his mother's presence, too.

Together, the bears ran through the darkness, heading toward the line of gold where the sun was just starting to rise.

LOOK FOR

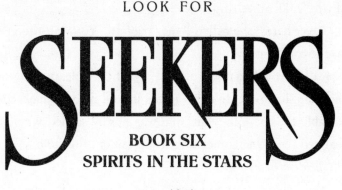

SEEKERS

BOOK SIX
SPIRITS IN THE STARS

Kallik

A glimmer of satisfaction crept through Kallik as she and her friends returned to the frozen sea. *They don't understand this place. I have to look after them.*

She had grown used to being the leader, the one who took charge of hunting and finding good places to sleep.

Now she was focused, intent on keeping their little group together as she scanned the sky for the lights that showed the presence of the spirits. But there were no lights. Their absence was a pain clawing deep into Kallik's heart.

Where are you, Nisa? Have you abandoned us?

"I'm so hungry!" Lusa exclaimed.

"I'm starving, too," Toklo grumbled.

"Kallik, can you find a seal hole?" Ujurak asked. His tone was edgy and his claws scraped impatiently on the ice.

"I'll do my best," she promised.

The other three kept walking while Kallik cast back and forth on either side. Eventually she spotted the dark patch

1

of the seal's breathing hole.

"Over here!" she called to her friends. "You wait there; I'll do the catching."

Kallik crouched down at the edge of the hole, making sure that her shadow didn't fall across it, and made herself comfortable for the long wait. She was hardly settled when she realized there was something strange about this hole.

There's no fresh scent!

The only scent of seal was faint and stale, as if none of the creatures had been there for a long time.

That's odd.

The moments dragged by as Kallik waited beside the neat black circle. There was no sign of movement in the water, and no scent of seal. Now and again she cast a glance toward her friends, who were clustered a few bear-lengths away. Lusa and Toklo were talking together quietly; Kallik could read impatience in the twitching of their ears and the scrape of their claws on the ice.

Ujurak sat a little way away from them, his muzzle raised and his gaze scanning the sky. It was full daylight now, and the sun shone down, gleaming on the surface of the ice. Kallik longed for the night, when she would be able to see the Pathway Star, and maybe the spirits would return to guide them.

She made herself concentrate on the seal hole again, alert for the first swirling of the water that would herald the appearance of a seal. But everything was quiet. At last, in growing desperation, she peered down into the hole to see if she could spot moving shapes in the water. But she saw nothing except the shadows in the ocean.

"Kallik!" Ujurak's voice cut through her concentration. "We have to keep moving."

Kallik's first instinct was to protest, to beg for a little more time. But she admitted to herself that however long she waited, there wouldn't be a seal for her to catch from this hole.

"Okay, coming," she replied, heaving herself to her paws and flexing stiff muscles.

Returning to her friends, she saw how anxious Ujurak was looking, though he said nothing, allowing her to take the lead as they set off once more across the ice.

He angled his ears toward a smudge on the distant horizon. Kallik felt more hopeful at the sight, and all the bears seemed to find new energy now that they had something to aim for. Their pace quickened.

As she bounded along, Kallik could hear sounds that she hadn't heard for a long time: lapping water and the high-pitched creak of thin ice.

We're getting close to land again. Or is the ice melting? A sharp pang of foreboding stabbed through her like a walrus tusk at the thought of being cut off from land. Picking up Ujurak's urgency, she ran even faster. A low ice ridge blocked their path; she pushed upward with powerful hind legs, springing easily to the top.

Only a few pawlengths ahead, the ice vanished. A wide channel had been gouged through it. It was about the width of one of the no-claws' water-beasts, and the stink of burning oil fumes still hung about it, making Kallik gag.

"Stop!" Kallik froze as she barked out the warning. "Danger!"

Her friends scampered past her, bounding up to the very edge of the channel and peering curiously into the water. Kallik stayed where she was, her paws turned to stone. The channel reminded her too much of the place where she and Taqqiq had crossed, where Nisa had given up her life.

Toklo was balanced on the very edge of the ice. "We'll have to swim," he announced. "It's not as wide as the Great River we crossed before Smoke Mountain. It won't take long."

"No!" Kallik choked out the word. "We can't. It's not safe."

Toklo narrowed his eyes at her. "Not safe how?"

Kallik swallowed. "Orca," she whispered. She stared down at her paws, struggling with terror.

Lusa padded over to her. Kallik felt the comforting warmth of the black bear's pelt pressed up against her own. "That's how your mother died, isn't it?" Lusa murmured.

Kallik nodded.

"I know how you feel," Lusa went on, her voice warm and sympathetic. "But it will be different this time. Everything will be okay. It's not far, and we'll swim fast. Besides, we're much bigger than you and Taqqiq were back then!"

You're not, Lusa, Kallik thought. *Maybe that seal hole was empty because there are too many orca here.*

Lusa gave her a gentle nudge, and Kallik allowed herself to be coaxed as far as the water. Peering into it, she saw that the edge of the ice was broken up where the water-beast had plowed through, and the reek of oil was stronger than ever.

"Kallik, we have to go this way," Ujurak said.

"He's right," Toklo agreed. "It'll be dark soon, and we can't stay here all night."

"I'll find a good place to slide in," Lusa announced, scampering along the ice at the very edge of the channel.

Suddenly there was a loud crack and the ice underneath Lusa's paws shattered, pitching her into the sea. Kallik started toward her, only to halt as Lusa's black head bobbed up again.

Lusa spat out water, her forepaws working vigorously. "Great spirits, that's cold!" she exclaimed. "But I'm in now. I may as well keep swimming." Facing forward again, she paddled strongly across the stretch of water, and Toklo slipped in after her.

"You next, Kallik," Ujurak prompted.

Kallik realized there was no point in arguing. She launched herself into the channel, and the water closed around her, cold and familiar. Behind her she heard Ujurak slide in and start swimming. Ahead, she could see that Lusa was doing well, already halfway across the channel with Toklo just behind her.

Suddenly Kallik spotted a flicker of movement in the corner of her eye. Turning her head, she saw a huge black fin sliding through the water, bearing down on Lusa. The little black bear swam on, unaware of her danger.

"Orca!" Kallik yelped. "Swim faster!"

WARRIORS

SUPER EDITION:
SKYCLAN'S DESTINY

Floodwater thundered down the gorge, chasing a wall of uprooted trees and bushes as if they were the slenderest twigs. Leafstar stood at the entrance to her den and watched in horror as the current foamed and swirled among the rocks, mounting higher and higher. Rain lashed the surface from bulging black clouds overhead.

Water gurgled into Echosong's den; though the SkyClan leader strained her eyes through the stormy darkness, she couldn't see what had happened to the medicine cat. A cat's shriek cut through the tumult of the water and Leafstar spotted the Clan's two elders struggling frantically as they were swept out of their den. The two old cats flailed on the surface for a heartbeat and then vanished.

Cherrytail and Patchfoot, heading down the trail with fresh-kill in their jaws, halted in astonishment when they saw the flood. They spun around and fled up the cliff, but the water surged after them and carried them yowling along the gorge. Leafstar lost sight of them as a huge tree, its roots high

1

in the air like claws, rolled between her and the drowning warriors.

Great StarClan, help us! Leafstar prayed. *Save my Clan!*

Already the floodwater was lapping at the entrance to the nursery. A kit poked its nose out and vanished back inside with a frightened wail. Leafstar bunched her muscles, ready to leap across the rocks and help, but before she could move, a wave higher than the rest licked around her and caught her up, tossing her into the river alongside the splintered trees.

Leafstar fought and writhed against the smothering water, gasping for breath. She coughed as something brittle jabbed inside her open mouth. She opened her eyes and spat out a frond of dried bracken. Her nest was scattered around her den and there were deep clawmarks in the floor where she had struggled with the invisible wave. Flicking off a shred of moss that was clinging to one ear, she sat up, panting.

Thank StarClan, it was only a dream!

The SkyClan leader stayed where she was until her heartbeat slowed and she had stopped trembling. The flood had been so real, washing away her Clanmates in front of her eyes. . . .

Sunlight was slanting through the entrance to her den; with a long sigh of relief, Leafstar tottered to her paws and padded onto the ledge outside. Down below, the river wound peacefully between the steep cliffs that enclosed the gorge. As sunhigh approached, light gleamed on the surface of the water and soaked into Leafstar's brown and cream fur; she relaxed her shoulders, enjoying the warmth and the sensation of the gentle breeze that ruffled her pelt.

"It was only a dream," she repeated to herself, pricking her ears at the twittering of birds in the trees at the top of the gorge. "Newleaf is here, and SkyClan has survived."

A warm glow of satisfaction flooded through her as she recalled that only a few short moons ago she had been nothing more than Leaf. She had been a loner, responsible for no cat but herself. Then Firestar had appeared: a leader of a Clan from a distant forest, with an amazing story of a lost Clan who had once lived here in the gorge. Firestar had gathered loners and kittypets to revive SkyClan; most astonishing of all, Leaf had been chosen to lead them.

"I'll never forget that night when the spirits of my ancestors gave me nine lives and made me Leafstar," she murmured. "My whole world changed. I wonder if you still think about us, Firestar," she added. "I hope you know that I've kept the promises I made to you and my Clanmates."

Shrill meows from below brought the she-cat back to the present. The Clan was beginning to gather beside the Rockpile, where the underground river flowed into the sunlight for the first time. Shrewtooth, Sparrowpelt, and Cherrytail were crouched down, eating, not far from the fresh-kill pile. Shrewtooth gulped his mouse down quickly, casting suspicious glances at the two younger warriors. Leafstar remembered how a border patrol had caught the black tom spying on the Clan two moons ago, terrified and half starving. They had persuaded him to move into the warriors' den, but he was still finding it hard to fit into Clan life.

I'll have to do something to make him understand that he is among friends now, Leafstar decided. *He's more nervous than a cornered mouse.*

The two Clan elders, Lichenfur and Tangle, were sharing tongues on a flat rock warmed by the sun. They looked content; Tangle was a bad-tempered old rogue who stopped in the gorge now and again to eat before going back to his den in the forest, but he seemed to get on fine with Lichenfur, and Leafstar hoped she would convince him to stay permanently in the camp.

Lichenfur had lived alone in the woods farther up the gorge, aware of the new Clan but staying clear of them. She had almost died when she had been caught in a fox trap, until a patrol had found her and brought her back to camp for healing. After that she had been glad to give up the life of a loner. "She has wisdom to teach the Clan," Leafstar mewed softly from the ledge. "Every Clan needs its elders."

The loud squeals she could hear were coming from Bouncepaw, Tinypaw, and Rockpaw, who were chasing one another in a tight circle, their fur bristling with excitement. As Leafstar watched, their mother, Clovertail, padded up to them, her whiskers twitching anxiously. Leafstar couldn't hear what she said, but the apprentices skidded to a halt; Clovertail beckoned Tinypaw with a flick of her tail and started to give her face a thorough wash. Leafstar purred with amusement as the young white she-cat wriggled under the swipes of her mother's rough tongue, while Clovertail's eyes shone with pride.

Pebbles pattering down beside her startled Leafstar. Looking up, she saw Patchfoot heading down the rocky trail with a squirrel clamped firmly in his jaws. Waspwhisker followed him, with his apprentice Mintpaw a pawstep behind; they both carried mice. Leafstar gave a little nod of approval as the hunting patrol passed her. Prey was becoming more plentiful with the warmer weather, and the fresh-kill pile was swelling. She pictured Waspwhisker when he had joined the Clan during the first snowfall of leaf-bare: a lost kittypet wailing with cold and hunger as he blundered along the gorge. Now the gray and white tom was one of the most skillful hunters in the Clan, with an apprentice of his own. He even had kits, with another former stray named Fallowfern.

SkyClan is growing.

Waspwhisker's four kits bounced out of the nursery as their father padded past, and scampered behind him, squeaking. Their mother, Fallowfern, emerged more slowly and edged her way down the trail after them; she still wasn't completely comfortable with the sheer cliff face and pointed rocks that surrounded SkyClan's camp.

"Be careful!" she called. "Don't fall!"

The kits had already reached the bottom of the gorge, getting under their father's paws, cuffing one another over the head and rolling perilously near to the pool. Waspwhisker gently nudged the pale brown tom, Nettlekit, away from the edge.

But as soon as their father turned away to drop his prey on the fresh-kill pile, Nettlekit's sister Plumkit jumped on him. Nettlekit swiped at her, as if he was trying to copy a battle move he'd seen when the apprentices were training. Plumkit rolled over; Nettlekit staggered, lost his balance, and toppled into the river.

Fallowfern let out a wail. "Nettlekit!"

Stifling a gasp, Leafstar sprang to her paws, but she was too far away to do anything. Fallowfern leaped swiftly from boulder to boulder, but Waspwhisker was faster still, plunging into the pool after his kit. Leafstar lost sight of them for a few heartbeats. She watched the other Clan cats huddled at the water's edge—all except for Shrewtooth, who paced up and down the bank, his tail lashing in agitation. Leafstar purred with relief when she saw Waspwhisker hauling himself out of the river with Nettlekit clamped firmly in his jaws. The tiny tom's paws flailed until his father set him down on the rock. Then he shook himself, spattering every cat with shining drops of water. Fallowfern pounced on him and started to lick his pelt, but Nettlekit struggled away from her and hurled himself straight at Plumkit.

"I'll teach you to push me in the river!" he squealed.